Lucas Wanted To Kill The Man Who'd Stolen His Wife From Him.

But with Kincaid already dead, vengeance was beyond reach. Or was it?

Why give up an eleven-year-old vendetta just because he wouldn't get to see his enemy writhe in defeat? He could still have the satisfaction of knowing he'd won, and that was what really mattered.

He stared at the door Nadia had slammed in his face. He could still have the pleasure of holding all his nemesis once possessed. Beginning with Nadia.

Dear Reader,

Life has a way of throwing curveballs when we least expect or need them. When I sold the idea for this book over a year ago, I had no idea how much life would imitate art or that I'd be walking in my heroine's shoes in many ways.

But life's curveballs are not all bad. They have a way of challenging us and making us grow—usually for the better, even though the process might have a few less than enjoyable moments.

When Nadia Kincaid's world is turned upside down she has two choices: quit or rise to the challenge. She makes the choice we all need to make when faced with a crisis. Watching Nadia find her feet and discover her inner strength has been an inspiration for me. I hope that if you find yourself on the receiving end of one of life's challenges you too can rise to the occasion.

Happy reading!

Emilie Rose

EMILIE ROSE

WED BY DECEPTION

Published by Silhouette Books
America's Publisher of Contemporary Romance

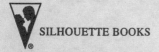 **SILHOUETTE BOOKS**

ISBN-13: 978-0-373-76894-3
ISBN-10:   0-373-76894-X

WED BY DECEPTION

Copyright © 2008 by Emilie Rose Cunningham

Recent Books by Emilie Rose

Silhouette Desire

*Paying the Playboy's Price #1732
*Exposing the Executive's Secrets #1738
*Bending to the Bachelor's Will #1744
Forbidden Merger #1753
†The Millionaire's Indecent Proposal #1804
†The Prince's Ultimate Deception #1810
†The Playboy's Passionate Pursuit #1817
Secrets of the Tycoon's Bride #1831
**Shattered by the CEO #1871
**Bound by the Kincaid Baby #1881
**Wed by Deception #1894

*Trust Fund Affairs
†Monte Carlo Affairs
**The Payback Affairs

EMILIE ROSE

Bestselling Silhouette Desire author and RITA® Award finalist Emilie Rose lives in her native North Carolina with her four sons and two adopted mutts. Writing is her third (and hopefully her last) career. She's managed a medical office and run a home day care, neither of which offers half as much satisfaction as plotting happy endings. Her hobbies include gardening and cooking (especially cheesecake). Her favorite TV shows include *Grey's Anatomy, ER, CSI, Dancing with the Stars, American Idol* and Discovery Channel's medical programs. Emilie's a rabid country music fan because she can find an entire book in almost any song.

Letters can be mailed to:
Emilie Rose
P.O. Box 20145,
Raleigh, NC 27619
E-mail: EmilieRoseC@aol.com

To Jules (aka Mari Freeman), a truly amazing friend
who's been rock solid by my side through the hard stuff.
I couldn't have done it without you, girl,
and "thanks" is woefully inadequate.

Prologue

"**A**nd last but not least, to my daughter, Nadia...'" Richards, the longtime family attorney paused in reading Everett Kincaid's will and sought Nadia Kincaid's gaze across the long dining-room table.

Every muscle of Nadia's body tugged as taut as a ship's anchor line in a swift current. She and her overbearing—now dead—father had shared a love-hate relationship, and in her opinion, the terms in his twisted will she'd already heard were going to ruin both her older brothers' lives for the next year. She dreaded finding out how dear old Daddy planned to mess with her head.

When Richards realized he had her full attention his eyes returned to the thick document. "'Your work record is commendable and your dedication to Kincaid Cruise Lines can't be faulted...'"

Nadia stiffened even more.

Not good. When her father started with a compliment he
always ended with an insult. He liked to lift you up so you
had farther to fall when he took you down.

"But your job and your empty-headed friends are all
you have. You surround yourself with people who give
no thought to the future, who never consider what they
would do without their trust funds and never plan
beyond their next party."

Nadia winced at the accuracy of his assessment. Her father
wouldn't understand that she liked her narcissistic friends
because they were too busy worrying about their own
neuroses to be interested in hers.

"You're twenty-nine, Nadia. It's past time you grew up,
took responsibility for your actions and discovered
what you want out of life. With that in mind, I'm
pushing you from the nest."

A frisson of alarm crept down her spine. "Pushing me
from the nest? What does that mean?"

"'Effective immediately,'" Richards resumed reading,
"'you are on an unpaid leave of absence from your position
as Director of Shared Services at Kincaid Cruise Lines and
you are banned from all KCL properties and Kincaid Manor.'"

Confusion swirled inside her like a riptide. What would
she do? Where would she go? With the stroke of his pen her
father had taken away her job, her home and any sanctuary
she might seek elsewhere. Why?

"'You will reside in my Dallas penthouse for 365 consecutive days.'"

"Daddy owns—*owned*—a Dallas penthouse?"
Richards held up a silencing hand.

"You are not allowed to seek other paid employment or to host parties in the apartment. I expect you to fill your days with a new class of people. And to make sure you're not partying with wastrels every night you must be in the penthouse between the hours of midnight and 6:00 a.m. every night."

Nadia snapped her gaping mouth shut. "Midnight? What am I? Cinderella?"

"'If you fail to fulfill my terms to the letter,'" Richards droned on in his usual monotone, "'then you will lose everything. And so will your brothers.'"

Her brothers. She forced her gaze from the attorney to Mitch beside her then Rand seated farther down the Kincaid Manor dining-room table.

"Can you believe this? He's grounding me and sending me to 'my room,'" her fingers marked quotes in the air, "as if I were a child." She folded her arms and sat back in her chair. "This is ridiculous. I'm not doing it."

"You have no choice," Mitch said quietly, calmly. Typical Mitch. Coolheaded in a crisis. She ought to know as many times as she'd dialed his number.

"Come on, Mitch. I can't give up my job, my home and my friends."

"Yes, you can." Rand leaned forward in his high-backed chair and rested his clenched fists on the table. As the oldest he'd been the one Nadia had always gone to with her troubles—before he'd abandoned her and KCL five years ago without a backward glance.

He held her gaze with his serious hazel eyes. "You heard Richards. If you don't, we lose everything. Mitch and I will help you."

"How? You'll both be stuck here in Miami while I'm banished to Dallas."

"Dallas isn't exactly the Arctic Ocean. We can get supplies in and out." Mitch gave her shoulder a gentle squeeze. He'd been her rock since Rand took off, the one she could count on…no matter what.

"But this is stupid."

Richards cleared his throat. "There's more."

How much worse could it get? Nadia's nails bit into her palms. She took a bracing breath and nodded for the attorney to continue.

"You have been pampered for far too long. Unlike your brothers, you have never even attempted to live in the real world outside Kincaid Manor—not even during college. It's time you learned to take care of yourself, Nadia, because your brothers and I won't always be around to clean up your messes."

Shame burned her face. Okay, so she'd asked for help a few times. Big freakin' deal.

"You will have no maid, no cook and no chauffeur."

Her lungs constricted and her head started to spin. Forget the fact that she'd probably starve, she hadn't had a driver's license before the accident, and she'd had no reason to get one after it. She sprang from the chair before the memories could seize her brain and paced a circuit around the room.

"A car and driving lessons will be provided for you. In addition, you will learn to survive on a monthly stipend of two thousand dollars."

"He's giving me an allowance?" she all but shrieked. She spent more on a single outfit.

"Because you're living rent free, that amount should be more than sufficient to cover your basic needs, pay your utilities, et cetera. A budget should help you understand KCL's employees and client base better."

He didn't think she could live on a budget? Okay, so, no, she'd never had a personal one, but how hard could it be? She was a trained accountant, for pity's sake, and she handled the multimillion-dollar KCL budget on a daily basis.

"This is crazy. Was Daddy out of his mind? Can he do this?"

Richards's bushy eyebrows hiked like thatched cabana roofs above his half-glasses. "One can do whatever one wishes with his or her assets. Your father is not asking you to do anything illegal or immoral. Need I repeat that if you fail, you and your brothers will forfeit your shares of Everett's estate and all of your father's holdings? Kincaid Cruise Lines, Kincaid Manor, each of the properties Everett owned around the globe, as well as his substantial investment portfolio will be sold to Mardi Gras Cruising, KCL's strongest competitor, for one dollar. And you will be left with only your personal funds."

Of which she had none. Thanks to her frenetic attempts to keep her mind and body occupied until she crashed into bed each night from sheer exhaustion, she lived pretty much from paycheck to paycheck.

"No. You don't need to repeat yourself. Dad has made it very clear that if any of us fails, we all lose. Everything. But why Mardi Gras? Dad hated that company with a passion. So do I. Their devious, underhanded, cutthroat tactics have cost us a substantial market share."

Richards shrugged. "Everett didn't share his reasoning on that issue with me."

Rand's fingers drummed the table. "Nadia, as much as I love the idea of Dad rolling over in his grave when Mardi Gras paints its logo on each of KCL's ships, I don't want the bastard to win this time."

Beside her Mitch nodded. "Agreed. We have to fight. It's too big a prize to hand off by default."

She knew very well there were billions at stake. She studied her brothers. Rand might have moved on and made a life for himself elsewhere, but Mitch lived and breathed KCL. Like her, he'd never worked a day for any other company. KCL was his universe, and she couldn't be responsible for taking that from him.

She could see by the resignation on their faces that Rand and Mitch expected her to botch this. That stung. But then what had she ever done for her brothers? They were always doing for her with nothing in return.

She knew what her father was up to. This was another test. Everett Kincaid excelled at testing his children—especially her because she reminded him of his dead wife. He'd always believed Nadia would crack eventually—like her mother had. Why else would he have forced her to endure more than a decade of therapy and now a year of solitary confinement?

But she'd prove him wrong. She'd prove them all wrong.

She would survive a year without her job, her friends and the safety net of her family. What choice did she have? Her brothers had been there for her when her life went so terribly wrong eleven years ago. She owed it to Rand and Mitch to come through for them now.

Her father obviously expected her to be the weakest link. But he'd be disappointed. She wasn't going to fail. She'd show Everett Kincaid his only daughter was made of sterner stuff. Because she hadn't just inherited her daddy's head for business, she'd also inherited his stubborn streak.

She could do this.

No. She *would* do this.

She would simply have to find a way other than submersing herself in work and partying to keep the haunting memories at bay.

Squaring her shoulders, she lifted her chin and locked her quaking knees. "When do I leave?"

One

As silent as a tomb. And after eight weeks of playing Suzy Homemaker, Nadia Kincaid felt as if she'd been buried alive in the luxurious penthouse.

Nice crypt, but still…a crypt.

She didn't even have neighbors as a distraction. The only other apartment in the downtown high-rise had been unoccupied since she'd moved in and the floors below were filled with businesses that didn't appreciate her popping in to visit. Not even when she brought the results of the new cookie recipes she'd tried.

She folded her dust cloth, parked her hands on her hips and stared at the shelves filled with books and videos Rand had sent. She'd promised herself she'd stand on her own two feet in Dallas, and she hadn't wanted to accept her brothers' help, but she also hadn't wanted to starve. So she'd caved and accepted his gifts. With the aid of the tapes and books and cable TV, she'd taught herself to cook. And since cooking was messy, she'd also learned to clean. She'd even managed to master laundry and all those other little things that had always been done for her as a Kincaid heiress. She was proud that she'd only had a few minor mishaps.

So there, Daddy. Two months and I'm still standing. Bet you didn't expect that.

She'd caught up on practically every movie and bestseller released in the past decade and even found a grocery store that delivered to downtown Dallas. Delivery, she'd discovered, was cheaper than taking a taxi to and from the store.

The only challenge she hadn't yet met was the driving lessons. She wasn't ready to get behind the wheel of a car.

Look how much damage she'd done from the passenger seat.

The memory sent her scrambling for a distraction the way it always did when the past slipped from its sealed vault. Whipping her rag back out, she dragged it across the polished granite mantle and focused on her anger toward her father.

He'd underestimated her *again* by giving her this stupid penthouse-sitting, find-herself, real-world job while giving her brothers more meaningful tasks.

Rand had been forced to return to Kincaid Cruise Lines and step into their father's shoes as CEO after a five-year self-imposed exile. Mitch would be playing daddy to their father's illegitimate toddler. But Mitch hadn't been forced to give up his job as the CFO.

She got to watch her nails grow.

But grief underlay her anger like silt at the bottom of a river waiting to be stirred up by a change in current. And her thoughts, like river water, turned murky at the oddest of times. Such as now.

Yes, she was furious with her father for treating her like

an inept child, but she also ached with the knowledge that there would be no more head-butting arguments with him, no more irate confrontations because he'd gone over her head or behind her back and undermined or overridden her decisions at work. There'd be no more fighting over the business section of the paper during breakfasts at Kincaid Manor, no more appropriate-behavior lectures and no more looking up at work or at a society event and knowing he was watching her every move. Watching and waiting for her to screw up and need bailing out.

Three months ago she'd been chaffing at his smothering surveillance and, yes, she admitted grudgingly, over the years she'd done some outrageous things just to get a rise out of him. Now she missed knowing she mattered to someone. Sure, her brothers cared, but they had their own lives and having her disappear for a year was no great loss to them.

But you don't want anyone to get too close. Caring means losing and losing means hurting.

And self-pity is pathetic. Get over yourself.

But she'd swallowed all the domestic goddess junk she could handle. Her brain was atrophying. What else could she do? The will stipulated she couldn't get a job, but she needed more to fill her days than cooking, cleaning and sitting on her butt with a book or movie and waiting for a sound from the hall.

No doubt the security guards and Ella, the neighbor's maid, thought she was stalking them since she rushed out to chat each time she heard the elevator doors open.

She glanced at the window but her own reflection on the darkened glass stared back at her instead of the lush greenery and bright flowers and tomatoes filling the trio of container gardens Mitch had sent her. Her gaze bounced to the grandfather clock. Eleven? Where had the day gone? Without a job to report to every morning and some social event to occupy her evenings time seemed to slip away from her.

Slowly, like a receding ice cap.

She had to find a new hobby, but it would have to wait until morning. And she wasn't going to call anyone else for help. She had to work this one out for herself.

What could she do to fill the hours before even the chance of sleep would come? With the time difference, it was too late to call her brothers and get an update on their romances. Both had fallen in love during her solitary confinement, and Rand and Mitch were well on their way to fulfilling their parts of the inheritance clause. Their happiness only reinforced the fact that she couldn't mess this up. Success or failure now rested solely on her shoulders. Her father and brothers expected her to make a mess of this, but instead she was going to be the one to nail the deal.

She nodded with a whole lot more confidence than she felt and selected a kickboxing workout video. If she did the routine twice, the exercise ought to tire her out.

Trying to work up some enthusiasm, she headed for the DVD player. A muffled thump stopped her. Had it come from the hall? If so, it was far too late for the neighbor's twice-weekly maid, and since security in the building was tighter than the Pentagon, it wasn't likely to be a prowler.

So what was it? Grumpy, aka Gary, the night security guy? He usually covered the Monday night shifts. The guy really didn't like her much. None of the security team did.

But this wasn't Grumpy's usual time. She headed for the foyer and squinted through the peephole.

Across the wide hall a tall, blond guy had his back to her as he shoved a key into the apartment door. His tailored dove-gray suit encased broad shoulders, slim hips and long legs. He carried an ostrich attaché case in his left hand and a Louis Vuitton garment bag sat to the right of his feet.

Her absentee neighbor? Hallelujah. Someone new to talk to. She yanked open the door. The man spun around swiftly as if she'd startled him.

No. It couldn't be. Nadia recoiled, stumbling backward. The doorjamb banged her spine. The pain barely registered. Her heart slammed. Her head spun.

No.

Not Lucas.

Lucas is dead.

But the man in front of her was a dead ringer for her dead husband.

"Nadia?" said an oh, so familiar voice.

Black spots danced in front of her eyes. A cold sweat coated her skin. She gasped for air and clung to the door frame.

"Nadia, are you all right?"

She couldn't move. Couldn't breathe. Couldn't blink. Transfixed, she stared at the apparition wavering in front of her.

"Put your head down."

The briefcase thumped to the floor. A strong hand cupped the back of her neck and forced her chin toward her chest. Her legs folded. She went down hard on her knees. Her forehead pressed the Aubusson rug while her thoughts tumbled out of control.

You've done it. You've finally cracked up. Just like your father expected you to.

When you open your eyes, you'll see a stranger. Not your dead husband. Or maybe nobody at all.

But the firm, warm hand on her nape felt very, very real.

And very familiar.

When the hall around her no longer tilted and whirled she batted that big hand away and eased upright.

Blinking didn't change a thing. The man kneeling beside her still looked like Lucas Stone. His tawny hair was shorter, expensively razor cut instead of the basic barbershop job she remembered. His face was leaner and scored by a few more lines, but those were Lucas's silvery-blue eyes. That was his slightly canted-to-the-right nose and his stubborn square chin.

"Y-you're dead."

The corners of the mouth she'd once loved to kiss turned downward and his eyes narrowed suspiciously. "Not the last time I checked."

"Daddy told me— I missed the memorial service. I— He said you died. From injuries sustained in the wr-wreck."

Scowl deepening, the Lucas look-alike sat back on his haunches. "Kincaid told you I was *dead?*"

Her tongue was as dry as driftwood and about as lifeless. She swallowed and nodded.

"Son of a bitch." He shot to his feet and offered her a hand.

She hesitated, staring at those long fingers, one of which had worn a shiny new gold band the last time she'd seen him— a ring she still kept in her jewelry box at home. Reaching for that imaginary hand would be like buying into this delusion. She rose slowly without assistance and scanned the hall for the guys in white coats. But she saw only the empty private penthouse elevator through its gaping doors.

"This isn't real. You're not real. Tomorrow I'll wake up and—"

The blond illusion followed her into the apartment.

Oh, God. She needed to call her shrink.

You fired him last week, remember?

Oh, yeah. Oops. Big mistake.

"I can't believe your father told you I was dead. What else did he tell you?"

She grappled to make sense of her delirium. "N-nothing."

He stopped a yard away and she caught a whiff of... Kenneth Cole Black?

Did hallucinations have a scent?

Tentatively, she reached out. Her trembling fingertips didn't sink into nothingness. They encountered a firm chest encased in a pale blue silk shirt. She flattened her hand on that make-believe chest beside the navy-and-pewter striped silk tie. The steady thud of a heart bumped against her palm.

Real.

He's not dead.

Lucas isn't dead.

Joy burst through her, warming her, whipping her already racing heart into a wild thrashing rhythm. She was halfway to leaping into his arms and wrapping her legs around him the way she used to but her euphoria sputtered then crashed and burned like a spent firework.

Wait a minute.

She punched his upper arm. The pain radiating from her knuckles definitely wasn't a figment of her imagination. "If you're not dead, that means you dumped me, you jerk."

"You wanted me gone," he countered calmly, evenly.

She gaped. "Are you crazy? I risked disinheritance to marry you. Why would I want you gone?"

"Your father said you regretted your 'little rebellion.' You'd decided slumming wasn't for you, and you were embarrassed by your working-class husband. You demanded a divorce."

Was that true? Had her father lied to Lucas and deliberately separated them? "I did no such thing."

"He also claimed you couldn't stand the sight of me because—" A muscle ticked in Lucas's angular jaw. His eyes filled with sadness, but his gaze didn't waver. "Because I killed our child and with it any feelings you'd ever had for me."

Her eyelids fluttered closed as an arrow of sorrow punctured her heart. Her breath hitched and her throat tightened. She pressed her hand to her stomach—her empty, flat stomach—gathered her courage and looked into the face she'd once adored.

"Lucas, you didn't end our child's life. I did." Saying the words she'd never dared admit to anyone else hurt worse than she'd anticipated.

His face blanched then turned granite hard. "What are you saying? What did you do, Nadia?"

The coldness in his eyes and voice surprised her. Comprehension dawned and the hairs on her arms and the back of her neck rose. "You think I deliberately ended my pregnancy? I would never…" She shook her head at the appalling idea. "I meant I caused our wreck."

The rigidness eased from his shoulders. "I was driving."

He blamed himself? She wouldn't wish that agony on anyone, especially when she knew where the real fault lay. How many times had she cursed herself for trying to seduce her new husband on the way to their honeymoon hotel? How many times had she wished she'd waited ten more minutes to get amorous? Her selfish lack of concern for anyone around them had changed everything. *Everything.*

In seconds she'd gone from holding the world in her hands to realizing what mattered most was something no amount of money could buy and her daddy couldn't fix.

"I had my hand in your pants."

Grief deepened the lines bracketing his mouth. "I missed the stop sign."

"Because I was distracting you." She curled her fingers around his forearm, needing to reassure herself that this wasn't a dream. The muscles flexed taut and hard beneath his sleeve. "Lucas, I was in a coma for a week. If I didn't ask to see you it's because I couldn't."

He searched her face as if seeking the truth, then rage flooded his eyes with shocking swiftness. "The lying, conniving bastard."

"Who?"

"Your father." Lucas expelled the words on a breath filled with pure hatred and his lips flattened into a thin seam.

Everett Kincaid had done a lot of rotten things in his time, and he'd been clear in his intentions to disinherit Nadia if she went through with the wedding. He'd even refused to attend the small ceremony. But after the accident he'd acted as if that threat had never been voiced. She'd believed it was because in almost losing her he'd realized he loved her.

She should have known better. Her father never backed down or admitted he was wrong. He'd seen Lucas as a mistake and, like all her other mistakes, he'd "fixed" it in his own way. The wrong way. She shouldn't be hurt or surprised her father had lied to Lucas and sabotaged her marriage. But she was.

What surprised her even more was that Lucas had let him. She'd thought Lucas was the one man strong enough to stand up to her father. "If you'd loved me, you would have come to see me anyway."

The jaw muscle twitched faster. "I couldn't."

"*Please.* You were the most determined person I'd ever met. I don't believe you couldn't find your way to my hospital room. I was in intensive care hooked up to a billion machines. It's not like I could run and hide."

He broke eye contact for the first time and presented her with his back. His shoulders looked as rigid as a ship's girder and definitely wider than when they'd last been together.

He clenched his fists by his side. "I was paralyzed from the waist down. The doctors told me the odds of me walking again were slim to none."

Her mouth opened, but she couldn't get her vocal cords to work. Her gaze traveled down his broad back. Lucas had been so virile and active. In fact, it had been his incredible body that had initially attracted her attention the summer he'd worked with the Kincaid Manor landscaping crew.

"You must have been terrified over the possibility of being unable to help support your mother and sisters."

Lucas turned and she didn't like the hard, uncompromising look on his face. "Your father said you couldn't handle being saddled with a cripple."

He'd ignored her comment, but she let it pass. She'd never met a man who liked to admit fear or weakness. "And you believed him? You didn't trust that I meant it when I promised 'for better or worse'?"

"You'd been a pampered princess all your life. Did I think you'd want to live in poverty and play nursemaid to a guy who couldn't even piss by himself? No."

She flinched at his crudity and his assessment. Then anger pulsed through her veins. Why did the men in her life always assume she was a useless screwup?

Okay, so maybe she'd made a few silly mistakes, but still… Her father and Lucas had no right to make a decision of this magnitude for her.

"You should have given me the chance to prove myself instead of presuming I'd fail."

She looked him over, trying and failing to imagine him

helpless. From what she could see he was even more muscular and fit than he'd been eleven years ago. And unless she missed her guess—which was unlikely because she knew her designers—his suit was Hermès and the shoes, Prada. Either Lucas wasn't a struggling landscape worker anymore or he'd come into some serious money. "You're not paralyzed now."

"Thanks to a series of surgeries and months of rehab."

"And you're here." She waved a hand to indicate the opulent penthouse level. "Why are you here?"

Did she imagine his hesitation or that he'd shifted his weight on his feet? "I own the building and I live across the hall."

"You *own* a fifty-story piece of prime real estate in downtown Dallas?" Definitely serious money.

"Yes." The pride and confidence in that single word were unmistakable. "Why are *you* here?"

"This is—*was*—my father's place."

His eyes narrowed to silvery-blue slits. "My attorney sold this apartment to an investment company CEO."

"No, my father bought the property under a dummy corporation he sometimes uses." Mitch had done a little digging after the reading of the will to discover that interesting tidbit. The question was, why had her father wanted to keep ownership of this place a secret from everyone including Mitch, his right-hand man?

Lucas snapped to attention and looked annoyed.

Then it hit her. The strength leeched from her legs. She leaned against the entry table. "My father engineered this."

"Engineered what?"

"This meeting. Dad died. His will requires me to penthouse-sit for a year. He must have known I'd eventually run into you. Why would he do that?" She paced a circle in the foyer, sneaking peeks at Lucas every few steps. What had the attorney said? Something about her father realizing he'd made some mistakes that he'd hoped to right. And look how his meddling had brought both Rand and Mitch love.

Surprise stopped her in her tracks. "Unless he's trying to get us back together."

Lucas snorted an unamused sound of disgust. "Not a chance."

"He must be. Daddy buying the apartment across the hall from yours in a building *you* own is too big to be a coincidence."

"Nadia, your father paid me to get out of your life and never contact you again. And he threatened to ruin me and my family if I did. He wouldn't try to hook us up."

Her stomach sank like the *Titanic* and a chill enveloped her like icy water closing over her head. Déjà vu. Buying off people was her father's favorite way to get rid of someone he found undesirable. He'd done it multiple times to both her and her brothers over the years.

"You took money to dump me?"

Lucas swiped his jaw with his hand. A dull flush covered his face. "He claimed that's what you wanted."

"How much?"

"Nadia—"

Her eyes and throat burned. A tremor worked its way outward from the frozen pit of her stomach. "How much did it take to make you forget me, Lucas?"

"I never forgot you. Or our baby."

"How much?" she repeated through clenched teeth.

His jaw shifted. "He covered the cost of my surgeries and rehab, and he offered tuition for my sisters and me to go to the colleges of our choice."

"Give me a number. I want to know *exactly* how much my love was worth to you."

He expelled a harsh breath. "Roughly, two million."

She closed her eyes as a fresh wave of pain, disappointment and betrayal deluged her. Her father hadn't intended this meeting to be a joyful reunion. He'd wanted to make sure she knew that the one man she'd worshipped, the one she'd kept on a pedestal for more than a decade as an icon of perfect love, was no better than the rest of the greedy schmucks who'd leeched off her or taken Everett's payoffs over the years.

Feeling sick, she wrapped her arms around her middle and turned away. Did no one love her more than money?

She'd thought Lucas had.

Wrong.

She'd believed him to be different from the hangers-on of her social circle who were only interested in what being with a Kincaid could get them.

Wrong again.

The knowledge made her feel small, insignificant and unwanted. And it hurt. God, it hurt. She'd loved Lucas enough to leave everything familiar and dear to her to be his wife.

And he'd betrayed her. He'd sold out.

Her father was right. Lucas had been her biggest mistake. And loving him and losing him had almost destroyed her.

"I wish you'd stayed dead." She pressed her fingers to the throb in her left temple and frowned at him. "No, I don't mean that. I just wish I'd never met you again. But let me tell you something, Lucas Stone. Choosing the money over me doesn't make you special or unique. It just makes you one of many and someone I don't want to know."

She had to get rid of him. Her legs shook so badly she barely made it to the front door without collapsing. "Get out."

"Nadia—"

"*Get out.* Before I call security."

"They work for me. They're not going to throw me out."
He closed the distance between them and stood toe to toe with
her, looming over her. "Don't blame me for your father's
machinations."

"This has nothing to do with my father who is—*was*—
without question an arrogant, manipulative, interfering ass,
and I hope he's roasting in hell at this moment. This is about
you. You betrayed me. You chose money over me and you left
me alone to grieve for you and our child. Do you know how
close I came—"

She clamped down on the words. No, she would never give
him that much power over her.

"You're a selfish, sadistic prick, Lucas Stone. And I don't
ever want to see you again. Leave."

He stared at her so long she thought she'd have to make
good on her threat and call for help. Although who she'd call
if building security wouldn't help was uncertain. Maybe her
brothers. No. She had to learn to deal with her own issues.

Finally Lucas brushed past her, shattering her heart all
over again.

Because losing him to death hadn't hurt nearly as much as
knowing he'd willingly left her…

As if she didn't matter.

Two

Lucas Stone wanted to kill the devious SOB who'd stolen his wife from him. But with Everett Kincaid already dead vengeance was beyond reach.

Or was it?

Kincaid, the bastard, may have been the ax man, but his sons, Rand and Mitch, had been equally convinced that Lucas wasn't good enough for their baby sister. They'd come to the wedding, but they'd made damned sure Lucas knew they were there to support Nadia and not because they approved of him.

Why give up an eleven-year vendetta when he could still have the satisfaction of proving the Kincaids had been wrong to write him off?

The clunk of the turning dead bolt lock jarred him clear down to his marrow. He stared at the door Nadia had slammed in his face. If anything, Nadia the woman was even more beautiful than the girl she'd been. Her hair was still a thick mass of shiny dark waves and her eyes were the same mesmerizing green, but her youthful softness had melted away to reveal exquisite bone structure. The kind of beauty that would never fade. Or so his mother had claimed after meeting her. His family had adored her—right up until she'd allegedly dumped him.

He didn't doubt Nadia's story. The shock and pain in her eyes had been too genuine. And it wasn't as if Kincaid hadn't tried to get rid of Lucas more than once before the wedding. Each time Lucas had been strong enough to resist.

But not that last time. Then he'd been weak. And he'd been afraid he'd become a burden to his already overtaxed mother, and he'd been pissed—seriously pissed—at Nadia and hurt by her apparent betrayal. He'd wanted to strike back in any way he could, and taking Kincaid's money had seemed like the only way available.

What Lucas didn't believe was Nadia's fairy-tale garbage about Kincaid's altruistic motives. If her father had arranged this meeting, it was to rub Lucas's face in what he'd lost not to reunite them.

The question was how had Kincaid discovered Lucas owned this building? Admittedly, KingPin Electronics, the listed property owner, was the most visible of his companies, but he'd intentionally kept his name off the letterhead and executives list. As with most of his companies, he guided his staff through conference calls and orders to his CEOs but rarely made a physical appearance. He kept his face and name out of the press.

His youngest sister called him "the submarine," and he liked the image of always lurking unseen below the surface while he got the job done.

He turned the key he'd left in the lock after Nadia's unexpected appearance, retrieved his bags and entered his apartment. He spent too much time in hotels and it was good to be home. His gaze swept his luxurious living room, each item tangible proof he'd hauled himself and his family out of poverty.

It was amazing how much ambition fury and hatred could generate. Over the past seven years he'd been stealthily stalking his prey, acquiring failing properties, turning them around and selling them at a profit until he had enough cash to ante his way onto Everett Kincaid's playing field. For the past forty months he'd specifically targeted the suppliers Kincaid used, bought them and upped the prices on the products KCL couldn't get elsewhere without a lot of aggravation.

Everett Kincaid had valued cold hard cash over anything and Lucas had been determined to bleed the man's vault dry. Until today, Lucas had also believed Nadia to be as shallow as her father, and he'd planned to make all of the Kincaids pay for treating him like garbage to be cast aside. For once he was glad to be wrong and that his disgust with Nadia all these years had been unjust.

He set down his bags and flipped through the mail piled on the hall table, most of it addressed to Andvari, Inc., which meant his assistant had stopped by the apartment.

The closer Lucas had come to reaching his goal of taking down Kincaid, the greater the need for secrecy, and four years ago he'd created the umbrella company of Andvari. Named for the Norse god who guarded his treasures with a cloak of invisibility, Lucas had made it impossible for anyone to penetrate the smoke screen and discover the true owner of Andvari and each of its multiple subsidiaries.

Or so he'd thought.

How deeply had Kincaid penetrated, and how had he acquired his information? Because without a doubt, as Nadia had said, her father's ownership of the other penthouse couldn't possibly be a coincidence.

He grabbed his suitcase, headed to his bedroom and slung the case onto the mattress. Just because Kincaid had denied him the pleasure of seeing defeat on his face didn't mean Lucas couldn't still have the pleasure of holding all his nemesis had once possessed.

Beginning with Nadia.

Wouldn't it be the ultimate revenge to win back the woman Kincaid had stolen from him?

Love had nothing to do with it. A lifetime of his mother and sisters and himself getting screwed over by that sappy emotion had killed any illusions Lucas had about lust and chemistry and the temporary insanity the combination evoked. Physically, he still wanted his ex-wife. But sex was all he wanted from her.

If there was any justice in this world, that bastard Kincaid would roll over in his grave the day his daughter remarried the man he'd fired and humiliated. It would be an even better day when Lucas Stone became owner of KCL, fired each of the Kincaids and covered each KCL logo with one of his own. And he would.

He didn't expect the job to be easy. But then nothing had been since he'd awoken in that hospital bed unable to feel his legs, see his wife or save his baby.

He whipped his cell phone from his pocket and hit his sister's number on speed dial.

"This better be good, Lucas. I'm in the middle of a hot date. My first in months," Sandi groused in his ear.

He glanced at his watch and grimaced. Almost midnight. "You still want that promotion you've been begging for?"

"Hell, yes. What's the catch?"

"I need time off."

"What's wrong?"

A valid question since he'd lived and breathed work since getting back on his feet. But if he came clean Sandi would get on the next plane to Dallas. "I need a break from the relentless travel."

"I don't believe that for one second."

"You don't have to believe me. Either you want the promotion or you don't."

"I do. I do. Hold on." He heard her muffled voice telling someone she'd be right back then what sounded like swishing sheets. He did not want to know about his sister's sex life.

A full minute later she asked, "What do you need?"

"Take over the Singapore account."

"Are you serious?" She sounded as shocked as she should be. This project was his baby. He'd already put pints of blood and sweat into it, but he should be able to safely hand it over now.

He loosened his tie and shrugged out of his jacket. "Buying up this loan is a big responsibility, but you can handle it. You're ready."

"Why are we incurring the debt?"

"I have my reasons. And I need you to keep any discoveries from Jefferson."

He knew his sister well enough to know the silence meant she was running through all the possible reasons he'd make such an odd request. "It's going to be hard to sign contracts without an attorney present. What gives?"

He wanted to evaluate the Kincaid-Jefferson connection before he went further. Chances were Jefferson had simply sold the apartment to a specific quality of buyer as he'd been instructed. But Lucas didn't want his attorney in on any more confidential dealings until he was sure there hadn't been any greased palms involved. Kincaid had been as crooked as hell and so were many of the people he'd associated with.

"I'd prefer to use another attorney on this one. I'll have someone on board before you fly out to meet with the executive committee."

"It isn't like you to pull a last-minute switcheroo. Why are you?"

He debated refusing to answer, but Sandi deserved the facts. "Jefferson sold Everett Kincaid the Dallas penthouse."

Seconds ticked past then she groaned. "It's Monday. Aren't you supposed to be in Dallas? Please tell me you're not going to get tangled up with the Kincaids again."

He ignored her question. No one knew his ultimate goal was to take down KCL and no one needed to. "I'll have the pertinent files couriered to you tomorrow."

"Didn't Everett Kincaid die a couple of months ago? That means... Lucas, tell me you aren't dealing with that selfish little bitch again."

His teeth clicked together. For the past eleven years they'd all believed Nadia a selfish bitch. He'd have to tell his family the whole story, but not before he verified a few facts. "If you want this promotion, do your job and keep your nose out of my business."

"I don't like this, Lucas. I don't like it at all."

"I don't pay you to like it."

Her ticked-off sniff traveled across the airwaves. "Do you want me to check into Jefferson's dealings?"

"I'll have Terri investigate. If there's a devious, dishonest man around, she knows how to find him."

Understatement of the year. At twenty-four his younger

sister had already married and divorced three of the lying snakes before wising up and turning her loser-seeking talents into a lucrative private detective agency, which Lucas had initially funded. He also employed his sister's firm to run background checks on every employee Andvari considered hiring. Could she have missed something on Jefferson?

"Just tell me the plan so I can prepare for cleanup detail."

"There won't be any cleanup. But if you must know, I'm going to get back everything Everett Kincaid took from me. Starting with my ex-wife."

Every part of the past eleven years had been a lie, Nadia concluded.

Her grief? For naught.

Her father's sympathy? Faked.

His concern for her well-being? Bogus.

Had everything he'd said and done since the accident been a bald-faced lie? Worse, she had believed in his sincerity, which made her a stupid, gullible fool. There must have been clues to his underhanded, twisted machinations. How had she missed them?

And who else was in on the deception? Had her brothers known Lucas was alive and profiting from her pain? Had her shrink?

She slammed the metal rectangular pan onto the granite countertop. The loud twang vibrated her eardrums. She braced her hands on the cool surface and bowed her head. How many people had been secretly snickering at her behind her back all these years?

She would find out. She might be hampered by her location, and her lack of funds, but she would identify each of the Judases before this year in exile ended. She couldn't return to Miami without knowing who she could trust and who she couldn't.

The doorbell peeled.

Glad of the distraction, she pushed off the counter, grabbed her money and hustled to the foyer. She couldn't finish the brownies until the store delivered her walnuts and a new bottle of vanilla. Baking kept her mind from slipping into the deep, dark, bottomless well she'd prefer not to fall into again. She'd spent too much time paddling in the murky depths already.

Who knew when she'd ordered the last batch of groceries that she should have specified the nuts already shelled? She'd never shelled a nut in her before-banished life, and a *Nutcracker* was the ballet she watched at Christmas not a kitchen implement—one of the few this kitchen lacked.

She didn't bother with the peephole since she was expecting her usual delivery guy and she'd told security to send Dan up as soon as he arrived.

But it wasn't Dan on her doorstep. Lucas stood outside looking totally *GQ* in Burberry. She couldn't get over seeing him in a suit instead of the snug T-shirts and jeans or khakis he used to wear.

The little thrill that streaked through her really ticked her off. "What do you want?"

His blue eyes ran over her like heated maple syrup over Belgian waffles, slowly slipping into crevices and beyond and making her hyperconscious of her sleepless night, the makeup she'd slathered on to cover the dark circles beneath her eyes and last season's less than stellar jeans and sleeveless sweater.

He pulled a bag with a familiar logo from behind his back and dangled it from one long finger. "Yours, I believe."

"Yes." She reached for it.

At the last second he snatched it away and sniffed. "Something smells good. What's your cook whipping up for lunch?"

"No cook. Me. Where's Dan?"

"If you mean the kid, I paid him. He's gone." He muscled past her into the apartment, and even though he didn't physically push her aside, his size, scent and presence had the same bulldozer effect of knocking her off balance.

"Come in," she sniped sarcastically. She didn't want him here, the traitor. She offered the folded twenties. "This should be enough to cover the total and the tip."

"I don't need your money. Is that marinara sauce?" He strode toward the kitchen as if he were familiar with the apartment's layout, which as owner of the building he might be. But even more irritating, he acted as if he had every right to venture where he pleased in her space. Which he most certainly did not.

Temper rising, she followed in the trespasser's wake. "Yes. I'm testing a new recipe and I'd like to finish it. So buh-bye."

She'd discovered if she didn't focus one hundred percent on the recipe, she'd mess up something, and sometimes it wasn't salvageable. Or edible. With her new budget she couldn't afford to throw out food—something she would remember next time she went to an overpriced restaurant and left most of her meal on her plate.

It'll be a long time before you hit another trendy restaurant. Forty-three weeks, to be exact.

Not a happy thought. Especially now that *he'd* turned up.

She reached for the bag again and again he eluded her. "May I have my groceries, please?"

"You couldn't cook eleven years ago." His gaze swept the homemade fettuccini waiting to be boiled and the bowl of unfinished brownie batter. He picked up the wooden spoon, stirred the pot then pursed his lips and sampled her sauce.

A territorial urge to growl rumbled through her. "Now I can. Lucas, I'm not interested in playing a childish game of keep-away. Hand over my nuts."

"Invite me to lunch." He scraped a finger along the edge of the brownie batter and licked the thick chocolate from the tip. "Mmm. And dessert."

That was not sexy. *It wasn't.*

She swallowed and closed her eyes against the shower of memories and hormones. Just because he'd had the most talented tongue on five continents didn't mean she wanted to experience his skills again firsthand. How could she ever trust him? She couldn't.

She planted her hands on her hips and scowled. "I don't want your company."

"You have more than enough for two and you know marinara is my favorite."

She'd forgotten. *Liar.* Okay, she hadn't. But she hadn't cooked the sauce for him. She liked it, too. It was the easiest recipe in the book and the only one she'd had all the ingredients for in the apartment. Besides, she'd needed something to go with the pasta she'd made using the machine Mitch had sent. Her brothers kept sending her kitchen gadgets to entertain her. Their help made being independent difficult. But it kept her sane. Catch-22.

"I'm freezing the leftovers for later."

His eyebrows lifted. "You're planning ahead?"

His incredulous tone ticked her off. "Is that so hard to believe?"

"Frankly, yes."

The sad fact was that two and a half months ago he would have been right. She hadn't planned ahead as her father had so unkindly pointed out.

She sighed and pushed back her tangled mop of hair, which only reminded her she would not survive a year without her hairdresser to keep the unruly waves under control. She'd have to find someone local. And cheap.

"Go away, Lucas."

He shrugged and headed back out the door—with her walnuts.

"Hey, hand over my groceries."

"You know the price," he called over his shoulder as he entered the open door of his place. Nadia plowed after him. She didn't bother to close her door because no one could get upstairs without security calling first, which was cool because it meant she didn't have to learn how to work the apartment's electronic security system. She just left it turned off.

"Lucas. Come on." Her steps stuttered to a stop inside his living room. She could see Reunion Tower through the windows on the opposite wall, but the landmark wasn't nearly as interesting as what lay on this side of the glass wall.

His place was even larger than hers. And more luxurious. Turning in place, she ran a quick mental tally of the imported carpets on the Brazilian cherry floor, the café au lait–colored suede sofas and chairs and the beveled glass-topped tables. Pricey. The original art on the walls hadn't come cheaply either. His decor screamed "I'm a success," but in an urban classic way instead of nouveau riche.

Wow. Someone had finally out-Kincaided her father who'd been a firm believer in appearances and accoutrements defining the man.

Lucas's living and dining areas made her want to see the rest of his place. But that wasn't going to happen. She wanted nothing—repeat, *nothing*—to do with Lucas Stone, the mercenary deserter.

"I can't finish my brownies without the ingredients in that bag."

"I like brownies."

She'd remembered his sweet tooth and his love of chocolate chip cookies. That's why she'd chosen to try baking brownies today instead of cookies. Besides, her Sub-Zero freezer was already full of cookie dough that she didn't know what to do with since she could no longer share it with the people downstairs.

She folded her arms. "I don't care."

He erased the distance between them, stopping only inches from her. Her senses went on full alert, but she stood her ground. Not even sheer will could stop her breathing and pulse rates from quickening, her mouth from moistening or her muscles from tensing.

Lucas lifted his hand and stroked her cheek before pushing a lock of hair behind her ear. That simple touch reverberated all the way to the pit of her stomach. Damn him. He knew her middle melted when he played with her earlobe like that. She jerked her head away from that lingering fingertip.

You are not attracted to him. Not anymore. You can't be.

"You care, Nadia. And from what the security team tells me you could use the company."

Heat steamed her face like a ship's boiler. "All I did was drop in downstairs to say hello."

"You made a nuisance of yourself until security escorted you from the premises and banned you from the lower floors."

Sad. But true. "I wasn't after company secrets. I wanted to share my cookies. I can't eat as many as I bake. It's not like I was trying to poison anybody."

"My employees don't need you telling them how to run a more efficient business."

Guilty. So she'd offered a few pointers… Wait a minute. Did he say— "Your employees?"

This time she knew she didn't imagine his hesitation or the slight narrowing of his eyes. "This building houses several of my companies."

"*Companies.* Plural? How many do you own?"

"A few."

Interesting. And vague. Deliberately? Definitely. She could see the guardedness in his baby blues. His evasion piqued her curiosity. Lucas had been ambitious before. But back then his goal had been to eventually own his own land-scaping company. He'd been attending college part-time in the evenings earning a degree in horticulture to help him.

She'd have to do a Google search on him as soon as she returned to her apartment and see what she could find.

"I'm good at what I do, Lucas. I could help."

"Get a job."

"I already have a job with KCL. Only Dad's stupid will has forced me to take a leave of absence, and I'm not allowed to—" she made quotation marks in the air with her fingers "—seek other paid employment."

His eyes narrowed. "Why?"

Oh right. As if she'd admit that her father had ordered her to grow up. "It's just his way of tormenting us from the grave. He assigned Rand, Mitch and me tasks we have to complete before we can settle his estate."

"What kinds of tasks?"

"None of your business. My life ceased to be your concern when you sold out."

The flare of his nostrils and compression of his lips told her she'd ticked him off. *Good.*

"What happens if you fail?"

"I'm not going to fail. If you remember, I can be quite persistent when there's something I want." Once upon a time she'd wanted him. But not anymore. "Now please, give me my food."

He kept the bag behind his back. Short of an undignified struggle, which would involve the kind of body contact she wasn't interested in, she couldn't retrieve it.

"Lunch...and dessert, Nadia."

The suggestive pause between the words combined with his deepening voice and the intent in his eyes made her heart thump harder. He wasn't talking about brownies. And her double-dealing hormones wanted to strip naked and dance around the room for him.

But that wasn't ever going to happen again.

"That seductive half smile is wasted on me, Lucas Stone. You've shown your true colors. I have enough backstabbing users in my life already."

Or she had before her father had cut her off from her "friends," none of whom had made an effort to call or visit her in Dallas. Would they even remember her when she returned home? Did she want them to?

"All I want is lunch and a chance to find out if our divorce is valid."

What? Her stomach hit rock bottom. "Why wouldn't it be?"

"If you believed I was dead, then why would you sign divorce papers?"

She winced and wished she could remember what—if anything—she'd signed. "Good point."

"Feed me and we'll talk."

When he put it like that what choice did she have? But first she needed to lock herself in a closet and scream bloody murder.

"Give me a minute." Nadia forced the words through the panic tightening her throat.

She bolted from Lucas's place and back to her own. She really, really didn't want to call Mitch to bail her out of this one, but if anyone could fix this the middle Kincaid—aka Peacemaker—could. She grabbed her cell phone and dialed her brother's direct line.

Her neck prickled. What if Mitch was in on the whole deceitful deal?

"Mitch Kin—"

"Lucas isn't dead," she blurted. "Did you know?"

"What?"

"He lives in the penthouse across the hall from Dad's and he owns this building. Did you know?" she repeated.

"Nadia, calm down. You're not making sense. Are you okay?"

She heard the concern in his voice elicited by the hysteria in her own and struggled to regain her composure before continuing. "I haven't lost my mind. Lucas isn't dead. Dad lied and he paid Lucas two million to dump me and disappear."

"That sorry bastard." She didn't ask whether he referred to her father or Lucas as the bastard. As far as she was concerned the term applied to both men. But her brother's shock and anger sounded genuine, giving her a small measure of relief. Maybe Mitch hadn't betrayed her.

"Mitch, Lucas made a valid point. If I thought he was dead, I wouldn't have signed divorce papers. I certainly don't remember signing anything. I need you to get your hands on whatever paperwork you can find that's related to my marriage, specifically the ending of it, and send me copies of everything. And I'm probably going to need a lawyer licensed to practice in Texas."

"Don't panic before we have all the facts."

"Don't panic? Are you kidding me? *My husband just rose from the dead.*"

Three

A hand plucked the cell phone from Nadia's fingers. She screamed, nearly jumped out of her skin and spun around to face her phone snatcher.

Lucas. She hadn't even heard him sneak up behind her.

"Hey! Give that back."

He ignored her and pressed her red phone to his ear—the same ear she used to nibble and whisper her most secret fantasies into. Right before he'd fulfilled each of them in sensual detail. She absolutely deplored the rush of heat that memory evoked.

"Mitch, this is Lucas Stone. After the accident your father told me Nadia insisted on ending our marriage. He had me sign divorce papers. If Nadia didn't sign the forms or didn't know what she was signing, we might still be married."

She couldn't still be married. She *couldn't*.

The strength and fight drained from Nadia's limbs. She

staggered to the kitchen and folded, as limp as freshly pressed pasta, into a chair. Parking her elbows on her knees, she plopped her head in her hands.

Lucas had to be wrong. Not just because of the things she'd done to try to forget him, but because she didn't want to be tied to a jerk who'd betray her.

Then there was the truth she'd discovered about her mother after the accident... Those facts changed everything. No matter what her shrink claimed, Nadia couldn't risk marriage. Not with her potentially defective genes.

And that wasn't the only thing that had changed. She pressed a hand over her navel and tried to convince herself that losing her baby had been a good thing given the circumstances. But as always, her pep talk fell flat.

Suddenly, her goal of getting through this year without botching the terms of the will or losing her mind seemed inconsequential. She had worse problems, specifically, the one that had followed her into the kitchen.

She dragged her gaze from his polished Guccis standing toe to toe with her Ralph Lauren sandals, up his sharply creased trousers over his lean hips and flat belly. Straightening, she snatched her phone from his outstretched hand before glaring at him. He'd ended the call without letting her say goodbye to her brother.

"If we're still married, I'll just get another divorce."

His mouth tilted into a see-if-I-care smile. "You're assuming I won't change your mind."

A sound of disgust gurgled in her throat. "Trust me, you can't."

Her unintentional challenge registered in his eyes and she wanted to kick herself for not choosing her words more carefully. She had brothers. She knew better than to throw down a gauntlet that way.

Lucas loomed over her, forcing her to lean way back in the chair and tilt her head to look up at him. His legs brushed her knees and her pulse rattled like a ship's dropping anchor chain. "Do you remember how good it was between us, Nadia?"

Heat blossomed inside her, unfurling like petals opening in the spring sunshine. She pressed her knees together to crush the ache between her legs and fought an urge to squirm in her seat.

How could she still desire him after what he'd done?

The memories of how it had been still haunted her. They hadn't been able to keep their hands off each other. Their passion had overridden everything—especially common sense—which was how she'd ended up pregnant within two months of meeting Lucas.

On her wedding day she'd been so full of joy, hope, excitement and love. They'd made love for the first time as husband and wife in an empty anteroom of his family's church with their guests only yards away because they simply couldn't wait. And despite, or maybe because of their cramped, illicit location it had been the most amazing sex of her life.

She squashed the memory and frowned harder. "That was a long time ago."

His direct gaze held hers. "Letting you go was a mistake. But I wanted you to be happy."

Snorting in disbelief, she shoved the chair backward and stood. "If you're trying to convince me you took that money for *my* benefit, you're wasting your breath. You won't get your hands on another dime of Kincaid money, so don't even think about asking for alimony if we have to redo this."

"I'm not interested in handouts."

"Even though a Kincaid handout bought you *this*." A snap of her wrist indicated his designer clothing.

"What I have now came from my own sweat. Your father's bribe was barely a drop in the bucket."

Two million was barely a drop? How loaded was Lucas?

He set the grocery bag on the counter, shrugged off his suit coat and draped it over the back of a chair. The David Yurman cufflinks he removed and dropped into his pocket were similar to the ones she'd bought Mitch for his birthday last year. He rolled up his sleeves revealing a Cartier Roadster watch on his tanned, hair-dusted wrist.

Oh, yes, Lucas had serious money these days.

But why was he undressing in her kitchen? "What are you doing?"

"Helping you cook."

"I don't need help." Not anymore. Thanks to her downtime in Dallas she'd become a freaking gourmet. But then she'd never done anything by half measures. If she jumped in, she tended to go for the deep end. What was the point in holding back when the things that mattered most could be snatched away in an instant?

"You're going to get my help and my company whether you want it or not." Lucas opened a cabinet door. Apparently not finding whatever it was he was looking for, he searched through another and another until he located her new pasta pot in a lower cabinet.

"You can't just barge in here and take over."

"Looks like I already have."

Daddy, if you weren't dead, I'd kill you for this.

"Then by all means make yourself at home in *my* kitchen." She served the words with a generous side of sarcasm and a mutinous glare.

"Do you have any red wine?"

"I don't drink."

Blue eyes nailed her to the travertine tiles. "That's not what the tabloids say."

Shame crawled up her neck and across her face. So she'd partied a bit over the past few years. But partying alone wasn't fun. It was pathetic. And she'd been alone in Dallas every day and every one of the past fifty-two nights.

"I was trying to forget my *dead* husband and the baby I'd miscarried."

Incredulity filled his eyes and slackened his jaw. "You expect me to believe you've been pining away for me for more than a decade?"

She squared her shoulders and sniffed. "Of course not. I had better things to do."

And if she hadn't, she'd never admit it.

He carried the pot to the sink and hit the faucet lever. While the water flowed he raided her cupboards, found salt and olive oil and poured both into the water without measuring.

She scrambled to her cookbook and scanned the recipe. A teaspoon of salt. Two tablespoons of oil. "How did you know to do that?"

He set the cookware on the burner and turned on the stove. "You've forgotten I grew up helping around the house. I learned how to cook as soon as I could reach the controls on the stove."

How could she ever forget that his loving family had been as warm and welcoming as hers had been cold and reserved? Or that she'd almost become a part of the Stones' tight-knit clan. And thanks to her miserable, meddling father and Lucas's greed she'd lost that chance.

Jerks. Both of them.

"How are your mother and sisters?"

"Fine." He moved to the knife and cutting board she'd left out in preparation for chopping nuts. A quick twist of his wrists tore the bag. He poured walnuts onto the white surface and started chopping quickly and decisively with far more skill than she'd managed to acquire.

Eleven years ago Sandi had been sixteen and Terri thirteen. They'd treated Nadia like the big sister they'd always wanted. And she'd loved it. "They must not think much of me if they believe I walked out on you when you needed me most."

"An accurate assessment. But they'll come around when we tell them the truth."

She'd often wondered why the Stones had never contacted her after the accident. Now she knew. And while she wanted to correct their opinion of her, it wasn't because she intended to allow Lucas back into her life. As soon as she got rid of him today she'd find a way to avoid him until he left town again.

"They don't need to come around."

He barely glanced up. "How many nuts do you need?"

"A cup." She carefully measured a teaspoon of vanilla and turned on the mixer to stir the fragrant liquid into the brownie batter. "Lucas, if we're still married—and I don't think we are because my father wouldn't make that kind of sloppy mistake—we are not staying married."

But her father had made a lot of mistakes recently, a nagging voice reminded her. Big mistakes. Like getting a woman her age pregnant and missing employees embezzling millions from right beneath his nose. Rand and Mitch were handling those messes without her and being excluded irritated her like a bad rash.

She tamped down the accompanying twinge of worry and reminded herself that her marriage *and its dissolution* had happened years ago when Everett Kincaid had still been at the top of his game.

Lucas dumped the nuts into the mixing bowl.

"Hey, you didn't measure. How do you know that's a cup?"

"Experience."

While she'd traveled the globe more times than she could remember before she'd turned eighteen, Lucas had been far more experienced than her in almost every other way eleven years ago, thanks to his less than stable upbringing. The contrast between his simple lifestyle and his savvy attitude had intrigued her.

He's not interesting. He's opportunistic. And don't you forget it.

She scraped the brownie batter into the pan then shoved the rectangle into the preheated oven.

Discovering she'd been living a lie had left her with a lot of questions—questions that had kept her up most of the night. She wanted answers even if it meant tolerating Lucas's company over lunch.

She propped a hip against the kitchen table, aiming for a casual pose when she was anything but relaxed. "What happened to you after the wreck?"

He leaned back against the counter and crossed his ankles. "Your father had me transferred to a Denver rehabilitation facility. He relocated my family and dumped his bribe into a bank account in my name. I studied while I was stuck in that wheelchair. Because of our background and our grades my sisters and I were able to get scholarships and financial aid to cover the majority of our tuition. I invested what was left after the medical bills and made it work for us."

"How?"

"I'm good with numbers." He pushed off the counter and gestured toward the steaming pot. "Water's boiling. Show me what you can do."

A blatant bid to avoid answering, but his tone carried just enough of a challenge to imply doubt in her cooking skills. She'd show him. And she'd get her answers. But first, she reread the last part of the recipe—just to be safe. She'd be darned if she'd have him looking over her shoulder correcting her "mistakes" the way her father always had. She began easing the pasta into the water.

"You took back your maiden name."

The statement made her hand slip. The remainder of the fettuccini plopped into the pot. Her hand shook as she very deliberately set the timer. She wouldn't tell him how numb she'd been after the accident or how little she'd cared what her name was or if anyone ever used it again.

"All my documents were in my maiden name. It was easier not to change everything over."

"The security team says you rarely leave the building. Why is that?"

She turned abruptly. He'd checked up on her? "I don't know anyone in Dallas."

"You know me. I'll show you the city."

"I don't want to go out with you."

"I know the best places to see and to eat."

Her mouth watered at the thought of eating something besides her own cooking or the occasional takeout.

"No, thanks."

"If you do nothing else, you need to see the gardens."

"Gardens are your thing, not mine." *Liar.* Lucas had taught her to appreciate more than run-of-the-mill shop flowers during their time together, and she adored puttering in the container gardens on her patio.

He'd taken her to Fairchild Tropical Garden in Coral Gables on their first date. Not a place to impress a girl, in her opinion, yet he had with his extensive knowledge of the exotic plants growing there. And, yes, okay, the flowers had been pretty and it had been interesting to actually see them in nature instead of in a vase.

Back then Lucas had been all about nature. On their second date he'd taken her to a state park. Initially, she'd been underwhelmed by his choice until they'd paddled around the marshes in a rented canoe talking, flirting and just enjoying each other's company without distractions. He'd shown her a side of nature not even the Audubon calendars could touch. And she'd loved it.

After they'd docked he'd cooked dinner for her on one of the public grills. She'd never had a man other than a paid chef prepare a meal for her before. It's no wonder they'd ended up making love for the first time that night in a campground cabin.

She was a Ritz kind of girl. If anyone had told her the most romantic night of her life would involve sitting on a fallen dead tree, listening to bugs chirp, wine with a twist-off top and dinner served on paper plates, she'd have called them crazy.

Not a memory she needed to wade through right now.

She yanked her thoughts back to the conversation. "It's July and it's hot. I don't want to tramp around outside. Especially with you."

"You never minded the heat before."

The lowered timber of his voice implied more than the temperature outside and rustled up memories of hot, sweaty outdoor sex. And hot, sweaty indoor sex.

She hustled to set the table. "You still like plants? I can't see you making the kind of money you'd need to buy a sky-scraper as a landscaper."

"I changed my major from horticulture to business."

"Why?"

His jaw shifted. "Because it wasn't practical to pursue a physically demanding career when I wasn't sure I could do the job."

Her breath hitched at the reminder of his injury.

The timer beeped. She knew from experience that home-made pasta disintegrated if she didn't get it out of the water promptly. Stifling her curiosity about the path he'd chosen, she strained the fettuccini, divided it onto plates then ladled sauce over it and set the dishes on the table. In the confusion of having him there she'd forgotten to steam the asparagus. Too bad. But giving him balanced meals wasn't her job.

She sat at the table, but the delicious aroma wafting up from her plate couldn't tempt her from what she really needed. "How long was it before you could walk again?"

He wound the noodles around the tines of his fork. "Fourteen months."

A long time to be scared. Sympathy softened her anger toward him. Unacceptable. *Don't forget he had your father's money to ease his worries. While you had nothing and no one. You'd lost your baby, your husband and had memories of your mother destroyed.*

"Eat your lunch, Lucas. I have plans this afternoon. And they don't include you."

Nadia opened her door Wednesday morning, bent to pick up her newspapers and froze.

Instantly on alert, she straightened, blinked to clear her

gritty, sleep-deprived eyes and reluctantly lifted her gaze. A dozen feet away *his* door stood open.

"Good morning," Lucas said the moment her gaze collided with his over the top of his newspaper. He sat in a chair that hadn't been in his spacious foyer yesterday with a coffee cup and two more folded papers at his elbow on the credenza. Judging by the way he'd left his door open and angled his chair to face her apartment the man was unabashedly waiting to pounce.

The delicious aroma of her favorite Jamaica Blue Mountain coffee crossed the hall to tease her nose. The rat. Her gourmet brew had been one of the first casualties of her new budget.

Determined to ignore him, she scanned the hall for her newspapers. All three were missing, and not once since she'd moved in had a paper been delivered to his door.

"You stole my papers."

"I'll share them with you over breakfast. C'mon over. We'll eat on the patio." He folded the paper and rose.

Her heart skipped at the sight of his muscled chest outlined to perfection by an Armani crew-neck black T and his long legs encased in low-riding black Prada jeans. The man knew how to dress his assets.

Quit gawking. Her molars clicked together. "I don't want to share my papers or breakfast with you. In fact, I don't ever want to see you again."

"So you said after lunch yesterday." He picked up the other newspapers and strolled deeper into his space.

She debated her options. She could slam her door and ignore him, chase him down and wrestle the papers from him, do as he'd asked or call her brothers and beg them to buy her an airline ticket home.

She sighed. While the last choice appealed the most, it wasn't going to happen. She had to stick this out. Shutting out Lucas literally and figuratively came in a close second, but one of the few things she had going for her in her exile was she finally had the time to stay current in world events by reading the papers cover to cover. She'd already lost touch with her life and her job. She wasn't ready to give up the outside world, and she could only take so much of the news channels' continuous looped coverage and cookie-cutter anchors.

That left options two and three. He was too big to tackle, which meant she had to endure his company. But if he expected her to change into something more attractive than her loose-fitting yoga pants and T-shirt or to put on makeup, then he was out of luck. She nabbed her cell phone from the hall table and padded barefoot across the hall, through his living room and out the glass door. The steamy Dallas heat instantly enveloped her.

His outdoor space, like the part of his apartment she'd seen, was twice the size of hers, and he even had a pool at the far end.

He dropped the papers on the table and faced her. "Why do you have a driving instructor waiting outside for you every day? One you ignore, I might add."

Her gaze snapped from the profusion of brightly colored potted flowers intermingled with odd-looking cacti to him. The security guys must have ratted her out. They'd get no more cookies from her. "None of your business."

"If you lived in Manhattan, I might understand why you don't have a driver's license. But most people in Miami drive. Why don't you?" He pulled out a chair at a glass-topped table set with dishes, a stainless coffee carafe and a heated, covered buffet server and gestured for her to sit.

"What makes you think I don't?" His knuckles brushed her back. She couldn't suppress a shiver. Darn him.

"I checked."

Anger burned a trail under her skin. "You have no right to invade my privacy."

"You live in my building. That gives me the right to do a background check." Leaning over her shoulder and invading her space, he filled a coffee cup for her, then circled the table and sat opposite her.

Okay, maybe he had a point. But she didn't like it. Squelching her irritation she lifted the cup, inhaled the rich aroma and sipped the dark, robust brew. Heaven. She might have to tolerate his company just for his coffee.

He removed the serving dish's lid revealing mushroom omelets, Canadian bacon and baked apples. The cinnamon and brown sugar scent made her mouth water. "Help yourself."

She usually skipped breakfast, but there was no way she'd pass up a meal she hadn't had to prepare and wouldn't have to clean up after. She filled her plate.

He passed her the newspapers and served himself. "You didn't answer my question."

"I never needed a license. I've always had a driver."

"You don't now."

She chewed slowly, trying not to let his statement ruin the delicious buttery taste of the eggs and melt-in-her-mouth bacon. She swallowed. When she, Rand and Mitch were younger a driver had been both a necessity and a security measure. Of course her brothers had rebelled over the restriction and gotten their licenses as soon as legally possible. But she never had because her father had been extremely overprotective. Then after the accident she hadn't even wanted to *ride* in the front seat of a car let alone drive one. Give her the backseat of a Lincoln or a limo any day.

She shoved the thought away and pressed a hand to the gnawing ache in her belly. Lucas might not have died, but her son had. "I guess your spies told you that, too?"

"My *employees* are paid to notice what happens on or around my property. I'll teach you to drive."

Her stomach knotted and her appetite fled. She halted her apple-laden fork an inch from her mouth and lowered the utensil. "No, thank you."

"You were studying for your driver's license exam before our wedding. Why didn't you pursue it?"

"I just didn't, okay."

"If you'd stayed married to me, you would have."

"Moot point. I didn't stay married to you. Your choice, remember?"

His eyes narrowed. He leaned back in his chair. "Are you afraid to drive?"

Her fingers spasmed on the fork. How could he know fear held her back? "Of course not. Don't be silly."

She hoped he missed the crack in her voice.

"You can't let fear rule your life, Nadia."

She couldn't quite meet his eyes and focused on the tip of his nose instead. "It doesn't."

"You claim your father's will requires you to penthouse-sit for a year. What happens if you don't?"

She would have been happy he'd changed the subject had he chosen any subject but *that* one. She abandoned her breakfast. "I'll fail to fulfill my portion of the inheritance clause."

"And then what?"

That her father was willing to give everything he owned

to his enemy rather than his own children was too humiliating to share. "I'll let everyone, but mostly myself, down."

Lucas laced his hands over his waistband. "Have you read your father's purchase agreement?"

She didn't like the sound of that or the intense look in his eyes. "No. Why?"

"Because as owner of this building, I reserve the right to evict any tenant with suitable grounds."

The scant amount of breakfast she'd consumed rolled in her stomach. What constituted *suitable grounds?* She needed to ask her lawyer what would happen if Lucas flexed his legal muscles. Would it set her free…or cost her and her brothers their inheritance?

Could she be held to the terms of the will if the apartment ceased to be available? And could her brothers blame her for aborting her portion of what Rand called the "inheritance curse" if it wasn't her fault? Or could they tie Lucas up long enough with legalese to get through the year?

Part of her hoped Lucas had just handed her an escape clause because she was afraid—very afraid—she wouldn't last another ten months in exile, especially with *him* here. But a small niggling part of her wanted to stay here and prove that she had what it took to stand on her own two feet simply because she was convinced her father and her brothers expected her to fail.

But until she could talk to Richards and find out where she stood she had to stall Lucas. "You can't do that."

"Either you take the driving lessons from me or I make a call to my legal department and you fail your brothers."

"What makes you think you're qualified to teach?"

"I taught both of my sisters."

"They didn't take Drivers' Education like normal people?"

"Our circumstances weren't normal."

Maybe not by his standards, but by hers his family had seemed perfect. Loving. Welcoming. Genuine. Sure, they'd been tight for money and they'd had their squabbles, but the love had been as sure as the sun rising. She hadn't had to wonder what the Stones really wanted from her or if they'd liked her. Every one of them had been an open book.

God, she'd missed them after the accident, but she hadn't had the guts to face them thinking they'd hate her for causing the wreck that had killed Lucas.

Which had turned out to be a total waste of worry on her part, hadn't it? They'd been living high off her daddy's money.

For now, however, what choice did she have but to accede to Lucas's stupid demand? Her cell phone rang before she could acquiesce. Glad for the delay, she snatched it up and checked caller ID. "It's Mitch. I have to take this."

She jumped to her feet and crossed to the far end of the patio and turned her back on Lucas. She stared into the clear water of the pool. "Mitch, what did you find out?"

"I found the divorce petition, but not the final decree. I'll keep looking for that. The petition is signed and looks official."

She exhaled in relief. "I don't remember signing anything related to my marriage, but you know how I was then."

"It was a tough time," Mitch replied. "We understood."

She'd been in a fog for months after the accident, going through the motions and barely functioning. By the time she'd pulled herself together she'd found herself enrolled in accounting classes at Barry University in Miami Shores instead of in New York City studying fashion design the way she'd always dreamed.

Had her father slipped the paperwork by her during that murky period? She hated that she'd been so out of it she didn't even remember. "When did I sign it?"

Papers rustled. "August 13."

Her blood ran cold despite the sultry morning. Mitch went on to rattle off other data from the form, but she barely registered what he said because it didn't matter.

None of it mattered.

Her heart hammered. She wanted to scream, *no*, but her lips moved without making a sound. She gulped air, fighting dizziness and nausea. "M-Mitch, that was four days after my wedding."

"Four days? But you were in a coma for—" Her brother's curses blistered her ear. Apparently Mitch wasn't always cool, calm and collected. That made two of them. "Your signature must have been forged."

Her thoughts exactly.

She tried to calm the horror streaking through her veins, but she was close to hyperventilating. "Does that mean what I think it means?"

"If your signature is invalid, then the document probably is, too, since no one had your power of attorney. I'll get Richards on it immediately. And we'll try to find the rest of the paperwork."

Her thoughts spun out of control as she mentally scrolled through the things she'd done to bury her grief. Things she wasn't proud of. Things a married woman shouldn't do. Because she'd felt dead inside and she'd needed to prove she hadn't died in that crash with her husband and son and because she'd felt she had nothing to lose. Life as she'd known it had ended.

She slowly turned. Her gaze found Lucas's across the patio and she couldn't look away.

"Nadia, don't panic." Mitch's avert-disaster voice didn't have its usual soothing effect.

"What do you mean *don't panic?* I'm still married to Lucas Stone."

Four

Still married.

Lucas couldn't hear Nadia's whispered words, but he could read her lips, see the alarm widening her eyes and the color draining from her cheeks.

He stifled the urge to pump his hand in the air and shout, "Yes!" as he crossed the flagstones. He stopped in front of her close enough for the morning breeze to carry her scent to his nostrils. *Her* scent. Not the pricy perfume she used to dab on interesting places. The memory of seeking out those intimate spots with his lips quickened his pulse. Nadia's fragrance still had the ability to rouse his hormones like nothing else.

She snapped her phone closed and took several deep, measured breaths, drawing his gaze to her breasts.

"Problem?" He kept his tone calm when he wanted to pepper her with questions, starting with what had Everett

Kincaid done wrong? But however his nemesis had screwed up this situation, Lucas wasn't above using it to his advantage.

And then there was the relief that neither of them had married in the interim. Bigamy wasn't pretty. His mother had discovered that firsthand.

Nadia blinked and swallowed and averted her worry-darkened eyes. Very telling. "There appears to be a glitch in the signatures on our divorce paperwork."

The barely detectable quiver in her voice was another giveaway. He knew he'd signed the forms, so his signature wasn't in question. "You didn't sign it."

"Um. I'm...not sure."

The truth was written all over her face. Nadia had never been able to lie worth a damn. Her honesty had been one of the things he'd liked about her...along with her traffic-stopping body, her I'll-try-anything-once sense of adventure and the warmth and openness she'd displayed toward his family. She had never seemed to look down on his mother despite the fact that Lila Stone had had children by three different men and had only been "married" to one of them—Lucas's good-for-nothing already married father who'd climbed into his eighteen-wheeler before Lucas's second birthday and had never come back.

Nadia's family hadn't been as accepting of Lucas. But they'd have to eat that attitude now along with a slice of humble pie when he took KCL from them.

"We're still married. That's what Mitch told you."

Her teeth pinched her bottom lip. "Maybe. He needs to do more research."

A gust blew a strand of long dark hair across her eyes. He lifted a hand and brushed it back, lingering on her soft cheek.

Her breath caught and her pupils expanded to almost obliterate her green irises. The chemistry between them hit him as hard as ever and it was clearly reciprocated. Getting her into bed shouldn't be too difficult.

She looked better this morning without the heavy makeup she'd slathered on her face yesterday. His gaze lowered to her unpainted lips. "Then by all means, let me kiss my bride."

He cupped her nape and covered her mouth with his. A charge of electricity arced through him. He relearned her softness, and with a sweep of his tongue across her bottom lip, her taste. For a second she leaned into him before she jerked out of reach.

Her arms flailed and her eyes widened. He grabbed her biceps to keep her from tumbling backward into the pool. For a moment he held her there, off balance and suspended over the water. Her pleading eyes locked with his, and then he swung her away from the lip of tile to safer ground.

"Careful."

She struggled to get free, but the flush on her cheeks told him she wasn't unmoved by the brief kiss.

"Let me go, Lucas. We are not resuming this marriage. Don't even think about it. My attorney will fix it." The moment he released her she put several yards between them.

Last time he hadn't had to chase her. Bold as brass, she'd initiated their first meeting and, yes, he knew it had been to piss off her father. Lucas had wanted her bad enough not to care. From that point on all he'd had to do was show up and let Mother Nature take her course. The attraction had been that strong. They'd spent every possible minute together.

It didn't look as though Nadia was going to make wooing her as easy this time around despite the still-strong pull.

"After you finish your breakfast I'll give you your first driving lesson."

"I don't want lessons."

He wasn't letting her off the hook that easily. "What's your job at KCL?"

She frowned as if having trouble following his line of thought. "I'm Director of Shared Services. Why?"

Surprise jolted him and reminded him he should have done his research on their executive board. But he'd had tunnel vision with Everett Kincaid as his target. He'd focused on KCL's data, assets and finances instead of personnel roster because he'd never once considered that Nadia might work for the bastard.

No doubt his finagling with KCL's suppliers through Andvari had been a thorn in Nadia's behind since her position was the one most directly burdened by his upping costs and making it difficult to obtain supplies. He'd have to keep that from her as long as possible or the spit would hit the fan.

"As upper management you know it would be bad PR for Kincaid Cruise Lines if word leaked out that Everett had frauded legal documents and bribed his daughter's husband to disappear."

She stiffened as she registered his implied threat. "You wouldn't do that. You wouldn't smear our names in the press and create a scandal like that."

He wasn't the boy she'd led around by the balls anymore. Life and Everett Kincaid had taught him some hard lessons and toughened him up. "Try me."

"Nadia, loosen your grip on the wheel."

Nadia glared at the man in the passenger seat of the Mercedes. She couldn't do as Lucas ordered. Her entire body felt locked, her muscles rigid with fear in the leather seats. And she couldn't stop shaking.

Her mother had died in a car accident. Her baby had died in a car accident. And until two days ago she'd thought her husband had, too. Seeing him in the flesh couldn't erase years of ingrained fear.

Irrational? Maybe. But she couldn't help the emotions churning through her.

She didn't want to be there. Not in Dallas. Not in this car. Not with this man—a man who had betrayed her and wasn't above using leverage to manipulate her.

Shades of your father.

On the other hand, she had to admit this hard-jawed, steely eyed, bossy, confident version of Lucas was…well, interesting in a way the younger man hadn't been.

Not that she'd ever get entangled with him again. And she certainly wouldn't give him another opportunity to grind her heart beneath his John Lobb shoes.

No matter how good he kissed.

The memory sent a flutter of something she wanted nothing to do with through her. Needing a distraction she scanned the vast, empty parking lot of the closed facility, hoping security or the police or somebody would arrive and throw them out.

She swallowed to ease her dry mouth. "We shouldn't be here. There were posted No Trespassing signs at the gate."

"It's private property. I know the owner."

"And would that owner be you?"

He paused as if considering his answer. "Yes."

"Why is the business closed?"

"You're stalling."

Smart of him to guess that. "And you didn't answer my question."

"The equipment is being upgraded this week. The plant will reopen on Monday. Start the car."

How hard could it be to turn the key? Impossible apparently since she couldn't relax her white-knuckled grip.

"Nadia, look at me."

She forced her gaze to meet his and found patience instead of irritation in his blue eyes.

"This is no different than driving the bumper cars at the amusement park. You enjoyed that. Didn't you?"

She inhaled slowly, calling upon the memories of happier times to wash over her. She and Lucas had spent a lot of time playing at the things normal people—not heiresses—did. He'd introduced her to a whole different world from the pampered, secluded one she'd grown up in. And he'd helped her fit in. "I did."

"Only this time you don't have to brace yourself because no one is going to bump into you. You have the entire place to yourself. Nothing bad is going to happen."

"Easy for you to say."

"You've driven golf carts. The pedals are the same."

She flexed her cramping fingers. The leather seats grew hot and moist against the backs of her legs.

"Nadia." His patience morphed into inflexible resolve. "We're not leaving until you've driven around the parking lot."

How stupid was it to not be able to drive a dumb car at her age? Definitely a sign of weakness. One she needed to overcome.

Everett Kincaid had abhorred weakness. No wonder he'd hung her out to dry.

"One time around the lot?"

He paused then dipped that stubborn chin. "Once around the entire property and then you can park the car."

One lap. She could do that. She turned the key and the motor purred to life. Her foot weighed as heavy as lead as she transferred it from the brake to the gas pedal. The engine roared, but the car didn't move.

"Put your foot back on the brake and put the car in Drive."

Idiot. But if Lucas thought she was lacking brain cells his even tone didn't show it. In fact, his soothing voice reminded her of the times he'd introduced her to other new things like riding a bicycle, free concerts in the park, making love on a blanket beneath the stars.

Don't go there.

Still trembling, she gritted her teeth and did as he instructed. The car inched forward. Her heart slammed harder, faster. She struggled to keep from hyperventilating.

She would get through this. And then maybe he'd leave her alone.

During her first two months in exile she'd prayed for her neighbor to come home. Now she couldn't wait to get rid of him.

Apparently, there was an upside to loneliness. And as soon as she ditched him she'd enjoy it, revel in it and be grateful for it. Screaming silences and all. No more whining self-pity.

"You're doing fine."

She glanced at him and her gaze snagged on his tender smile—the one that had haunted her dreams for years.

"Eyes on the road, princess."

She jerked her face forward again, but her pulse skittered anew at the old nickname.

"You have forward nailed. When you come around the backside of the building let's raise the bar and practice keeping the car between the lines."

He'd always done that. Encouraged without berating.

Guided rather than ordered. After her father's build-'em-up-to-take-'em-down MO she'd always braced herself after each of Lucas's positive comments eleven years ago. But the negative follow-ups had never come.

She didn't want him to be nice or patient or positive. She wanted him to be an obnoxious ass.

It'd be easier to hate him that way.

Because right now he was making that very, very difficult.

She'd never been more aware of a body in her life.

His or hers.

Nadia backed into the far corner of the elevator, as far from Lucas as she could get. She concentrated on the seam between the doors and tried to tune out the scent of the man standing two yards away. The man currently staring at her.

She sensed that blue gaze as surely as a touch and it made her skin hypersensitive. She could feel so much: the weight of each piece of clothing on her skin, the slight shift of her blouse with each breath she inhaled and exhaled, the tickle of her hair against her cheeks and nape. But along with the awareness and the wariness came a sense of accomplishment.

She'd driven a car.

That didn't mean she wanted to take one out on the road, but still…she'd made progress today that eleven years of therapy hadn't been able to accomplish.

Thanks to Lucas.

Don't go there. He's an opportunistic bastard. Remember?

She couldn't forgive him for choosing money over her, and she couldn't let her bitter feelings toward him soften. But she was in danger of doing both.

Replaying the too cozy dinner she'd just shared with him

at the steak house, the quiet conversation about art and music, movies and books was bad news. He'd put her at ease just as he had on their first date—the only date she'd ever been nervous about in her life. She couldn't dwell on the feeling of success she'd had when she'd mastered his car. Okay, *mastered* might be a slight exaggeration, but her one lap around the parking lot had turned into an hour once she got past her nerves.

And she certainly couldn't recall the good times they'd had together in the past.

She could feel herself weakening. She gave up and let her gaze meet his. The hunger burning in his eyes took her breath away. His gaze dropped to her lips which suddenly seemed dry and hot and swollen. She bit her tongue rather than dampen them.

She wanted him to kiss her. That would be a major mistake. His good-night kisses tended not to end before breakfast. That's how she'd become pregnant the first time. She searched for a diversion. "Thank you for dinner."

"You're welcome. We'll do it again soon."

Not a good idea.

"I'm proud of you, Nadia."

His quietly uttered words sent warmth rushing through her. When had anyone ever told her that? She gathered her wits. "I'm proud of me, too."

"You did very well for your first lesson. Tomorrow will be easier. Be ready at nine."

She winced. "About tomorrow…"

The elevator doors glided open, stilling her words.

Lucas shoved off the wall, but he didn't exit. He came toward her, closing the distance in three long strides. He planted one hand on the wall beside her head.

Her pulse thundered in her ears. She had to break this up. Fast. "Well, okay, thanks again for dinner. I—"

He nudged her chin with his knuckle. She couldn't breathe. God, she wanted him to kiss her. Instead she listened to the voice screaming caution in her brain, ducked beneath his arm and dashed out of the cubicle and to her door.

"I'll see you. Good night."

She hustled into her apartment and shut the door.

Close call. Too close. She had to get control of her hormones before they got her into trouble.

At one minute after six the next morning Nadia eased open her apartment door and peeked out. The hall was empty and Lucas's door was closed.

She had to get out of here.

She stepped over her newspapers rather than bring them in. Let him think she was still sleeping. She quietly closed the door and tiptoed toward the elevator. She'd yet to figure out how her father's minions—whoever they might be—would know if she wasn't inside between midnight and 6:00 a.m. It might be somehow related to the security system that she'd neglected to use even once since moving in. Whatever. She wasn't blowing her assigned task on a technicality.

The elevator opened with a ding. She winced, darted inside and hit the button to close the doors. Her muscles remained stiff with tension all the way down and as she exited the box and crossed the lobby.

"Going out, Ms. Kincaid?" the security guy asked.

She forced a smile and prayed he didn't have a concealed button to buzz his boss in the penthouse. "Yes."

"Would you like a taxi?"

"No, thank you, William."

Hurdle number one. If she wanted to travel under the radar, then she had to master public transportation. But if she could juggle the needs of dozens of ships navigating the globe, she could handle moving one person via a city rail system.

She'd printed a Dallas Area Rapid Transit map from her computer and tucked it into her oversize tote bag along with her laptop. The map and a loosely formed strategy should get her through today and keep her away from this building and its owner.

"You're getting an early start," William said, clearly hunting for information.

And the longer she stayed in the lobby chatting the better chance Lucas had of catching up with her and shadowing her. After yesterday's bonding experience and last night's near-miss kiss she didn't want that.

"Yes. I am."

"Headed anywhere in particular?"

She hadn't been born yesterday. If she told William where she was going, it would probably be relayed upstairs before her feet hit the sidewalk. "I plan to play tourist and see as much of the city as possible. Have a good day."

She plowed through the front doors and headed toward the transit station as quickly as her high-heeled Stella McCartney wedge sandals would take her. She hated liars and fibbing even though telling little white lies was de rigueur in her social circle.

The muggy morning air enveloped her as did the sounds and smells of early rush hour traffic. She was used to the bustle of big cities, but it was different somehow when you had only a general clue how to get where you were going and no driver waiting at the curb to carry your bags or give you directions. Or better yet, to drop you off at the door. She also tended to travel with a posse of friends—or leeches as her father would call them—who knew their way around.

Her plan: find an Internet café and drink coffee until the library's doors opened.

The *library*. She shook her head. Once upon a time she'd have killed time by shopping in Manhattan or Paris or Milan. But not now. Not with her budget and travel restrictions. She needed somewhere free and air-conditioned where she could pass the hours and keep herself too occupied to think about the ecstatic "welcome home" dance her hormones had done when Lucas's lips had touched hers.

She didn't spot anyone following her. Nevertheless, she squeezed into a group of a half dozen other people crossing the street trying to get lost in the crowd.

It might have only been sixty hours since her "dead" husband had risen, but she'd already figured out the Lucas of today wasn't the Lucas of her past. He wasn't going to jump when she crooked her little finger. And she wasn't sure exactly how far he'd go to make her fall in line with his plans. Whatever those were, she wanted no part of them…unless they included a new divorce. And that didn't seem to be on his agenda.

She observed the other commuters until she managed to figure out how to buy a day-pass ticket and then she boarded the train. It was disgusting how reliant she'd become on others for trivial but necessary details in twenty-nine years. Her father was right. She'd had no clue how to survive in the real world.

But she was going to learn.

She wasn't co-dependent at work. On the job she was more than competent. Just look how well she'd done these past three years with that damned Andvari challenging her every step. The company had made her job a living hell by stealing most of KCL's suppliers. She'd had to bust her butt to find the goods the cruise line needed at reasonable prices. Even her father hadn't been able to find fault with the creative solutions she'd presented to the Andvari problem.

But personally, well, she needed a little more work than a day at the spa could fix. And that was probably her father's point in exiling her halfway across the country.

Understanding his motives didn't mean she wasn't still peeved with him. Seriously she'd-never-forgive-him peeved.

The DART ride passed quickly and mercifully without incident. She even managed to get off at the right stop. After coffee and a fruit-yogurt-and-granola parfait she entered the library as soon as the doors opened. One whiff and she felt right at home. Nothing smelled like a building full of books.

Back during her college days she'd spent a lot of time hanging out in the stacks, studying and avoiding her father.

See a pattern here, Nadia? Her shrink's voice echoed in her head.

Hmm. She avoided the pushy men in her life by hiding out. Yes, definitely a pattern. One she needed to correct. And she would. As soon as she was on firmer ground. But for now she'd continue avoiding Lucas. And if he found her in this library, then Google said there were twenty-two others in the Dallas area and all had free Wi-Fi. She'd keep moving and try to stay one step ahead of him.

Speaking of Google, he'd had her so rattled she'd forgotten to do an Internet search on him.

With the first order of business determined, she found a quiet table tucked in the back and out of sight of the main entrance and booted up her laptop. She typed in *Lucas Stone* and hit Search.

There were several Lucas Stones, but none of them were

hers. Not hers. *Him,* she corrected. She tried a different search engine with the same results, then a third and a fourth. How peculiar. If the man owned businesses, he shouldn't be this hard to find.

She opened her e-mail account and typed in her brother's address. Mitch had resources she lacked. She composed a quick message asking him to check the apartment paperwork for an eviction clause and the will constraints to see if Lucas could indeed boot her out and what the consequences of that would be.

And then she made her last request.

As much as she hated asking for help again, she needed to know exactly who and what she was up against with Lucas Stone.

"You dodged your driving lesson."

Lucas's voice behind her in the apartment hallway made Nadia jump. She hadn't heard him open his door. She kept her back to him and turned her key in the lock. "Sorry. I had things to do."

"You failed to mention your busy schedule last night when I told you to meet me at nine."

Searching her brain for any excuse to get out of another evening in his company, she faced him. He wore faded jeans and a white V-neck T-shirt. Both Diesel. The man had learned how to dress his assets. And he had quite a few of them to display.

Ignore his assets.

"Probably because you ordered me to be ready instead of asking. You should remember that orders give me hives."

Her father had excelled at issuing commands and he'd expected unquestioning compliance. So, yes, she'd stood up to Lucas. Unforgivably rude of her, but given that the alternative of spending the day with him had been much more dangerous to her willpower, she'd decided a little discourtesy was the wiser option.

"You have five minutes to get ready for your lesson."

"Lucas, I'm tired. I've been out all day. I just want dinner and sleep."

"We have reservations after your lesson. You won't have to cook."

Another meal she wouldn't have to prepare. Tempting, but hadn't he heard a word she'd said? "And if I refuse?"

He pulled his cell phone from his back pocket.

He'd call his attorney or the press or…whoever could make her life the most miserable. 'Nuff said.

"It'll take me more than five minutes to get ready."

"Ten."

"Ten minutes? But—"

"Clock's ticking. We're running out of daylight for your lesson." His watch face glinted in the overhead lighting.

"Don't you have anything better to do than harass me?"

"What could be more important than reconnecting with my long-lost wife?"

"I am not your wife."

"Would you like to see the copy of the divorce petition and the final decree I received today? I compared your signatures to the ones from your old letters. The signatures on the legal documents are good copies. But they're not yours."

Just what she was afraid of. Mitch was supposed to be overnighting the paperwork to her so she could verify that fact.

Then Lucas's words registered. *Her letters.*

A flush warmed her from the inside out. He hadn't had Internet access back then so they'd corresponded the old-fashioned paper way. The notes they'd exchanged had been…racy to say the least. Full of fantasies and intent and raw emotion.

She'd kept everything he'd given her. Every letter. Every ticket stub. Every dried, pressed flower. These days the collection was buried in the back of her closet in Miami.

After Lucas's "death" she'd practically set up a shrine in her room for Lucas and their son. Her father had hated that. Now she knew why he'd badgered her so tenaciously to find someone new, rushing her past her grief until she'd struck back by deliberately bringing home the worst possible candidates, one after another, and flaunting them in her father's face until he'd quit nagging her.

But none of those men had ever been able to take Lucas's place or make the numbness go away. And none of them had been able to fill the void caused by the loss of her baby.

Lord, what if she had found someone? What if she'd married him? She shoved away the thought.

"You still have my old letters?" She'd lost count of the number of nights she'd slept with his clutched in her arms.

Memo to self: Throw the crap out.

"I kept them to remind me that some women don't honor their vows."

"But I—"

He held up a hand. "Your father screwed us both. I don't hold you responsible for that. Get moving, Nadia. You only have eight minutes left."

She stomped into her apartment and swung the door shut behind her. A boom jerked her around. Lucas had his palm splayed on the wood. He'd caught the door before it slammed in his face.

"I'll wait inside."

So she wouldn't change her mind and lock him out. Smart man to know the thought had crossed her mind. More than once.

She could argue with him, but what purpose would that serve? He had her with the dual threats of eviction and exposure and he knew it. She marched into her bedroom and locked that door before stripping.

She would not dress up for him. Instead she pulled on last year's black jeans and a lime-green XCVI shirt. The ruched knit top made her breasts look larger. She probably should have had them augmented like everyone else in her Miami circle, but she still had an allergy to hospitals. Couldn't get near one without feeling as if her throat had closed up and she was going to suffocate.

She checked the mirror and finger combed her desperately in-need-of-a-trim-and-highlights hair. Waking up from a coma with a shaved head and tubes coming out of every orifice had not been a pleasant experience. It had gone downhill from there when her father had told her about Lucas and their baby. And then a month later she'd learned the horrifying truth that her mother's death hadn't been an accident nor had it been Mary Elizabeth Kincaid's first attempt at suicide.

Once Nadia had climbed out of her deep pit of grief, she'd vowed to never allow herself to be that vulnerable again. And that meant not opening her heart to a man again—particularly the one in her living room.

Shaking off the memories, she freshened her makeup. She had enough pride that she couldn't go out looking like yesterday's news. She stabbed her feet into a pair of Michael Kors sandals and yanked open her door.

Lucas Stone could force her to spend time with him, but

he couldn't make her forget the hard lessons his disappearance had taught her.

Falling in love with him had been as natural as breathing and the easiest thing she'd ever done in her life.

Losing him had been the hardest. And it had almost driven her to follow in her mother's footsteps.

Five

A bloodcurdling scream to Nadia's right scared the *bejeezus* out of her. She jumped sideways in the semicircular restaurant booth and landed half in Lucas's lap.

She twisted toward the source. A woman in the next booth stared goggle-eyed at the man slumped beside her in his seat, his chest covered in red, his mouth moving soundlessly, his eyes wide and unfocused.

Horrified, Nadia glanced around. What had happened? Had he been shot? She hadn't heard a gun.

She gathered her composure. She'd been trained for disaster back in the days when she worked on KCL's ships, although she'd never had to deal with more than basic first aid. Peeling herself away from the heat of Lucas's body, she tried to slide from the booth to offer assistance. Lucas caught her wrist in a firm grip and held her back.

Heart pounding, she tugged her arm, but Lucas kept her

in her seat. "Let me go. I'm trained in first aid and CPR. I can help."

A smile lifted one corner of his mouth. Why was he smiling when the guy beside them could be dying?

"Nadia, it's a play," he whispered.

The woman at the next table covered her face and began to wail out nonsense, her loud voice echoing throughout the restaurant.

Useless idiot. Do something instead of just screeching.

But the increasingly hysterical woman didn't even try to staunch the bleeding and no one else came forward to help. Nadia snatched up her cloth napkin intent on putting pressure on the wound—wherever it was—and tried to rise again. The clamp on her wrist anchored her.

"Lucas, he needs medical attention. Call 911."

Lucas grabbed her shoulders firmly and forced her to look at him. "It's a play, Nadia. Mystery dinner theater."

She'd heard his low-pitched words, but they didn't make sense. She blinked, trying to comprehend. "What?"

"The victim and his date are both actors. You used to love Broadway. I wanted to surprise you with a show."

He'd surprised her all right. "A play?"

She glanced back over her shoulder to the other people coming onto the scene, their lines projecting to even the farthest table in the room.

A play. And Act I was unfolding right in front of her.

Now that she knew what she was looking at, it was obvious. Good acting, but still acting with the gestures and expressions a little grander than necessary.

Tension drained from her limbs. She felt like an imbecile as she watched the assembled cast go through their lines and hit their marks. Her racing pulse slowed but her face burned.

How many people had seen her try to charge to the rescue? Did everyone in the place except her know they were here for the entertainment?

She wanted to slide down by Lucas's side and hide.

As if he understood, he shifted, draping his arm across her shoulders and pulling her closer on the vinyl seat. He laced the fingers of his opposite hand through hers and rested their linked hands on his thigh. The electrifying warmth of his palm, his shoulder and his leg pressed against hers made her breath catch. And then his scent, his heat and his nearness converted embarrassment into awareness. Her heart skipped anew.

She attempted to pull away. He tightened his hold. She couldn't struggle or make a scene without drawing attention away from the actors who were finally moving en masse toward a stage that an opening curtain revealed.

"How did I miss the signs telling what this was?" she whispered.

He bent closer, his warm breath stirring her hair. "There weren't any posted signs. The place looks just like a regular restaurant."

His mouth brushed her ear as he spoke and then he sucked her earlobe between his lips. The jolt of arousal charging through her wasn't welcome. She wiggled, intent on putting space between them, but his iron grip didn't loosen.

"Be still. Enjoy the show."

What choice did she have?

She focused on the cast, some rising from other tables around them to join the action in front of her. A detective swaggered onto the set. Nadia tried to concentrate on the dialogue, the setting and the story. Anything to keep her mind off the man fused to her side.

She'd always been a huge Broadway fan and often jetted to New York to catch an opening, but she'd never done a dinner theater where the cast actually masqueraded as diners.

When she and Lucas had been dating he hadn't been able to afford Broadway tickets let alone the time off work to go to Manhattan. He'd introduced her to local theater and concerts in the park where more often than not they'd watched from a quilt on the grass. She'd loved the casual performances, but mostly she'd loved watching the entertainment from the vantage point of his arms. She was a little too comfy in those arms right now but another wiggle gained her no breathing room.

She pushed the memories away and immersed herself in the murder mystery until the curtain dropped for intermission. Lucas lifted their joined hands to his lips, jarring her back to the present. The soft brush of his mouth over her knuckles set her heart racing and ignited a flame low in her belly. Their gazes locked in the shadowy theater, and the urge to kiss him hit her hard and fast.

She adored the way he kissed.

"Enjoying the show?" he asked.

She needed to break the spell he'd cast over her before he had the chance to betray her again. But somehow she just couldn't make her body follow orders and instead, she caught herself leaning toward him. "Yes. Thank you for thinking of this."

"You're welcome." He released her hand and brushed back her hair, his knuckles skimming beneath her cheekbone in a caress that made her nerve endings quiver. The reflection of light off the polished crystal of his watch snagged her attention.

Time.

She'd lost track of time.

She bolted upright, grabbed his wrist and turned it so she could see his watch. She'd given up wearing hers weeks ago because awareness of the crawling minutes made the hours drag slower. And she'd had no need to worry about curfew since she didn't go anywhere.

Eleven-thirty. She was going to be late. Adrenaline rushed through her. She dropped his wrist and scooped up her purse. "I have to go."

The detective strolled onto the stage and began his monologue. She hated being rude and walking out in the midst of a performance, but her and her brothers' inheritance depended on it.

"The play's not over."

"I can't stay." She slid out of the booth and hurried toward the exit.

Lucas caught up with her in the lobby, gripped her elbow and pulled her to a stop. His blue eyes searched her face. "Nadia, what's wrong. Are you ill?"

The concern darkening his eyes and straining his face tugged at something deep inside her.

"No. But I…" How much did she want to tell him about her father treating her like a child by grounding her and setting a curfew? None of it. But again, her choices were limited. "Look, just take me home. Or if you want to stay and see the end, I'll take a cab. But I have to go. *Now.*"

"You were enjoying the performance."

"Yes, I was. The show is great. But I have to go."

"I'll drive you home if you level with me."

She hesitated. "Lucas, could we please have this conversation en route? I'll explain. I promise. But, please, get me back to the apartment. And hurry."

He crossed to the maitre d', said a few words and handed the man a couple of folded bills, then he returned to Nadia's side. "Let's go."

Dozens of phrases ran through her head as she hustled to the car. None sounded right, and she still hadn't come up with a suitably edited version of the disaster called her life by the time he'd pulled onto the highway.

He glanced at her. "Start talking."

She sighed. It should have been easy to confess the whole sordid mess in the darkened car, but she couldn't. "I have to be home by midnight."

"Why?"

"It's a condition of my father's will."

"And if you're not?"

"Things could get ugly. Not just for me, but for Rand and Mitch and Rhett."

"I've met Mitch and Rand, but who's Rhett?"

"My half brother. Dad surprised us with an illegitimate one-year-old son."

She had yet to see anything more than e-mailed photos of her baby brother. There hadn't been time to meet him or cuddle him before she left, and thanks to the stupid will she wouldn't get the chance before next June. By then he'd be two, no longer a baby and probably not interested in letting his estranged half sister hold him.

Rhett looked just like a Kincaid. Who would her son have taken after? Would he have been dark-haired and green-eyed like her or blond and blue-eyed like his daddy?

"How could it get ugly?"

Lucas's question hauled her from the deep well of what-might-have-beens. She debated how much to disclose and decided to keep it short. Need to know, as Mitch would say.

"If I don't follow the rules, I'll jeopardize our inheritance. I'm not going to do that."

"This is all about money?"

"No. It's about me coming through for my brothers for once instead of always relying on them." Oops. She'd said too much. She hoped he missed her slipup.

"Relied on them how?"

She winced. "They were there for me after you…died. I wasn't…in good shape. And I owe them this. I have to do my part."

Lucas muttered something that sounded like a curse under his breath. "Your father was a real piece of work."

"No kidding. And the more I learn—" She bit off the words.

"The more you learn…what?"

Lucas had been privy to too many of her rants about her father in the past to be surprised by the secret she'd never disclosed to anyone. Not even her brothers. "The more I wonder whether he loved me or hated me."

"Because you reminded him of your mother."

He remembered. She swallowed, trying to ease the lump in her throat and nodded. He took one hand from the steering wheel, reached across the center console and covered her fist and squeezed reassuringly.

"Hating you is impossible, Nadia. Believe me. I tried."

His words hit her with a punch of choking emotions. The scary part was the feeling was mutual. She couldn't hate Lucas, either. But she had to get over him and move on. Because her memories of the perfect love they'd shared were nothing more than fantasies.

True love didn't come with a price tag.

"We made it with five minutes to spare," Lucas said as Nadia shoved her key into the lock.

"I'm sorry I made you miss the ending of the play."

She opened the door and stepped inside, glancing around and wondering not for the first time if there was a camera or a trip switch or some other 007 gadget to register her comings and goings and whether she was solo or accompanied by a party. Or was her monitoring system something more basic, like her father had bribed the security staff? That would be more Everett Kincaid's style. Her father had always believed everyone had a price. History had shown he was usually right. Take Lucas, for example.

Wouldn't Lucas love knowing his team had sold out to her father? But she wouldn't voice her suspicions, because she wasn't sure what would happen if the reporting on her activities suddenly stopped. Her father's crazy will had left too many strings untied and too many questions unanswered. And all of the clauses were unbreakable, or so her brothers said. They'd each hired teams of lawyers to try to break the will with no luck. She hadn't had the cash to do so.

Now that she was back in her prison away from home, her heart slowed for the first time since she'd raced out of the restaurant. They'd had to detour around a traffic accident and she'd panicked, afraid of being late. She'd never had a problem with deadlines before. In fact, at work she thrived on them. But five minutes to midnight was cutting it too close for her peace of mind.

She turned in the foyer and startled at finding Lucas right on her heels. Close enough to touch if she wanted. And she didn't. Okay, yes, she did. And that wasn't good. Time to finish this before her weak will landed her in trouble.

"Thank you for the driving lesson, the show and dinner."

"We need to get an earlier start tomorrow." He moved forward.

She retreated. Avoiding him was still her number one

priority—especially after the understanding he'd shown tonight both during the driving lesson and when she had to leave the play. His compassion was eroding her defenses.

"Lucas, as much as I appreciate your help, I know you must have to work. Your businesses, whatever they are, can't run by themselves. I'll reengage the car company my father hired and finish the lessons."

And she would. Later. Thanks to Lucas getting her past her initial fear, she believed she'd eventually be able to get a driver's license at some point in the future. But not on busy Dallas roads. Best postpone the whole deal until she returned to Miami.

"Not necessary. I've got you covered." He advanced. The look of intent in his eyes sprouted goose bumps under her skin and doubled her pulse rate. Did he consider this a date and expect the traditional ending?

If so, she had to keep that from happening. She backed deeper into the apartment. "It's late. You need to go. Thank you again. Good night."

"Not yet." He captured her hand, dragged her into the living room and sat on the sofa. He tugged her down beside him. "Tell me what you did after the accident."

She did not want to have this conversation, but apparently giving him the postcard version was the only way to get rid of him. "I went to college. In the summers I worked for KCL."

"Doing what?"

"I worked on Crescent Key."

"The private island the cruise ships use?"

He shifted and his hot, hard thigh pressed hers. His lock on her wrist kept her from escaping. "Yes."

"Doing what?"

She tried to block the memories of being pressed against him without the hindrance of clothing. "I led kayaking and snorkeling excursions or filled in wherever else I was needed."

"Pretty good for a first job."

"Yes. You know Daddy wouldn't let me work before I turned eighteen."

"Nor did you want to."

"Well, no." Having a job had never occurred to her before she'd met Lucas. Why would it? She'd had more money than she could spend. But she'd been prepared to work after they'd married. She'd known Lucas couldn't afford for her not to. But she'd planned to get a job in a chic clothing shop.

Had he leaned closer? She arched her back to escape, but he pulled her forward and lowered his head. His mouth took hers before she could protest or evade him.

The kiss slammed into her like a rogue wave, towing her under in seconds. Under a deluge of memories. Under a somersaulting swirl of sensation. Under the spell he'd always been able to cast over her with no apparent effort. She clutched his upper arms to push him away, but ended up clinging for balance.

He didn't kiss the way he used to. Eleven years ago Lucas's kisses had been passionate, but teasing and tempting, luring her into love play. Tonight he kissed like a man on a mission to destroy each of her reservations.

And he was doing a damned fine job.

Pull away.

The contrast between the softness of his lips and the firm confidence in his possession robbed her of the ability to comply with the simplest of commands.

One arm tightened around her waist, bringing her torso

flush with his hard body. His other hand grazed up her side and her neck to cradle her jaw and tilt her head for deeper penetration. He sucked her bottom lip into his mouth and nipped gently, sending shock waves of arousal through her. The hot, slick, wet sweep of his tongue against hers dragged a hungry whimper from her throat and stirred a whirlpool of want in her midsection.

His taste filled her mouth, his scent her nose, and his big body seemed to surround her, making her feel protected and desired. Just like the old days. She fit against him as if she never should have left.

She'd missed this.

Her heart clamored out an SOS, her muscles weakened and her head spun. She clung to him because she couldn't possibly imagine doing anything else. His five o'clock shadow rasped her chin. Her fingers tightened and relaxed on his biceps like a cat's kneading paws. She couldn't help herself. She needed to touch him.

He shifted, laying her back on the cushions and following her down. His erection lengthened and thickened against her hip. And she wanted him. As much as she'd ever wanted anything. Maybe even more. But she couldn't have him. Not now. Not ever again. Because nothing was the same.

Nothing could ever be the same.

She ripped herself from his arms, sprang to her feet beside the sofa and pressed her fingertips to her mouth. She backed away. She stumbled over something and struggled for balance. Lucas stood and caught her, his grip firm on her elbows. She regained her footing, jerked free and looked down. Her purse. She didn't even remember dropping it beside the sofa.

That was twice she'd almost fallen and he'd had to catch

her. He kept her off balance mentally and physically. She had to be more careful around him or she was going to end up falling again. For him.

One glance at his desire-flushed face and passion-darkened eyes and a fresh wave of hunger swelled inside her. She had to look away and covered the action by bending and snagging the straps of her handbag. She slapped it down on the coffee table, marched for the front door and yanked it open. She focused on his left shoulder as he approached rather than his too-sexy face.

"I can't—I *won't* do this, Lucas. Please leave."

"You want me as much as I do you."

His husky tone made her nipples tighten. "I've learned the hard way that I can't have everything I want. Sometimes what I want isn't good for me."

Silence ticked between them.

"I'll see you in the morning, Nadia. Sleep well."

The second the door closed behind him she sagged in relief that he hadn't argued or tried to change her mind. She wasn't up for that—especially when she'd be fighting herself as much as him. And she wasn't sure who'd win.

But one thing was certain. This marriage was a no-win situation and she had to get out of it. Lucas had taken money to hurt her.

And she was damaged goods.

"Excuse me."

The hushed voice pulled Nadia's attention from the stack of fashion magazines on the library table in front of her early that Friday afternoon.

"Yes?"

A petite salt-and-pepper-haired fiftyish woman stood

beside her. Her glasses hung from a beaded chain around her neck. "Are you Nadia Kincaid?"

Nadia ignored years of ingrained caution and welcomed the interruption because the magazines weren't doing a good job of distracting her from the fact that her brother was getting married today, and she couldn't be there because she couldn't leave Dallas.

Damn you, Daddy.

Rand had promised to figure out a way to stream video of the ceremony through her computer tonight so she could "see" Mitch marry Rhett's aunt—a woman Nadia had never even met.

"Yes. I'm Nadia Kincaid."

"I thought I recognized you from your picture in a tabloid I found this morning."

Nadia fought the urge to shift in her chair. Her cheeks warmed. People were strange. She was no celebrity, but she'd been asked for her autograph before. It was a little weird, a little embarrassing, but it wouldn't cost her anything but time…of which she had a surplus since she was still avoiding Lucas until the last possible moment tonight. "Can I help you?"

"I'm hoping you can. Because you see…" The woman looked over each shoulder and leaned closer. "I read that rag before I recycled it."

Uh-oh. Was she going to get thrown out? And what crazy story had the tabloid "reporters" fabricated this time? She hadn't given them any ammunition to crucify her with lately.

"I'm Mary Branch, the head librarian here. The article says you orchestrated a fund-raiser for premature babies last spring in Miami and raised a record-breaking amount."

Tension relaxed its grip on Nadia's muscles and pride filled her with warmth. "Yes, I did."

She'd donated her time and her expertise at finding unusual, hard-to-get items for the auction because some preterm babies stood a chance. Hers never had.

"Our library fund-raiser chair stepped down unexpectedly this morning. Since I saw you in here yesterday and again today, I'm hoping you'll be in Dallas long enough to give us a few pointers…or whatever expertise you can spare. We're floundering without a leader. It's too late to cancel the event, not that we can afford to. The fund-raiser supports most of our programs throughout the year."

Since finding creative solutions to problems was her thing, Nadia couldn't help but be intrigued. "When is your event?"

"Three weeks."

Three weeks and they were a ship without a captain? Big challenge. "How much is left to be done?"

"I don't know. I have Sue Lynn's notes in my office. I could show them to you. If you're interested in the job, that is."

How many times would her father's stupid last requests come back to bite her? "I'd really love to help you in any way I can. But I can't accept paid employment because I'm on a leave of absence from my other job. However, I can volunteer my time."

"Your generosity warms my heart, honey. It's an absolute miracle to find someone with your expertise at such short notice. Would you like to take a look at those books?"

"Certainly." Nadia rose, a sense of purpose energizing her as she gathered her belongings.

The offer was the answer to her prayers. Helping with the fund-raiser would relieve her boredom and give her a legitimate reason to be out of the apartment and avoid Lucas Stone.

But most of all, it would give her a really good reason to stay in Dallas and something to think about besides her risen-from-the-dead husband—and the very good chance she would fail her brothers.

Six

"I don't care how hard it is to get," Lucas told his lawyer over the phone. "I want a copy of Everett Kincaid's will. Obtain it by any means necessary short of breaking in and stealing it."

A knock on his door surprised him. Nadia. It couldn't be anyone else. Security had buzzed him the minute she'd entered the express elevator. That she was seeking him out this time instead of making him hunt her down accelerated his heart rate and sent anticipation surging through him.

"I have to go. Call me when you have what I need." He disconnected.

Last night's kiss had made him more determined than ever to get his wife back in his bed. She wanted him. He'd tasted it on her lips, felt it in the melting of her body against his and the way her pulse had fluttered beneath his thumb. That's why he'd had her followed this morning. He'd needed to know where she was going and who she was seeing. He didn't play for keeps, but neither did he share his women when he was in a relationship.

He dropped the portable phone on the table, crossed the living room and opened his door. Nadia's flushed cheeks and sparkling eyes took his breath. Her wide, blinding smile nearly knocked him off his feet.

"I have a job."

The library. His behind-the-scenes maneuvering must have paid off. He made an effort to mask his satisfaction. "I thought you said you couldn't work because of the will."

"It's not a paying position. I'm volunteering to help with the library fund-raiser. Their chairwoman quit unexpectedly."

A free 'round-the-world cruise on Mardi Gras's most luxurious ship would do that to some people.

"She left them in the lurch and in a bind. The head librarian recognized me from an article she'd read about an event I chaired in Miami and asked me if I would be interested in taking over as the fund-raising committee chair."

Her obvious happiness hit him in an odd way, one he couldn't explain and didn't want to probe too closely. But somehow her good mood lightened the weight of his day's aggravations, and the excitement radiating from her eased his guilt for having manipulated the situation.

"You like fund-raising?"

He knew she did. He'd read the same article before sending it to the librarian along with the promise of a sizable donation if the library committee found Nadia a place in the group. He hadn't expected them to hand her the top position even though Nadia was well-qualified for it according to his research and the tabloid article.

He'd have had a better chance of forgetting her since the

wreck if those damned tabloids didn't relish reporting on the life of a shipping heiress. But funny how none of them mentioned she apparently worked as hard as she played. Terri's quick report on Nadia had revealed a dedication to her job and to raising money for an assortment of charities. His sister wasn't thrilled to be researching Nadia.

"I'm good at organizing and planning and finding needles in haystacks." Her confident statement and erect carriage reminded him of the old Nadia, the one he'd fallen in love with because she'd honestly believed she could conquer the world and change it.

That self-assured woman hadn't been in evidence since their reunion four days ago. Until now he'd seen no sign of the one who—even though he hadn't realized it was her— had countered his every move from her position as director of shared services when he'd tried to sink Kincaid Cruise Lines via their suppliers. He had to respect that kind of intelligence and determination. When this was over and he'd taken down KCL he'd consider offering her a job.

"The library is lucky to have you."

And he'd be fortunate she'd be occupied during the day because it would give him time he needed to help Sandi finalize Andvari's latest deal. His sister had run into a few snags she couldn't handle alone. Principally, an old-school banker who preferred women stay at home wearing an apron.

"I hope so. But I wanted you to know I'll be MIA for the next three weeks."

Not part of his plan. "Get home each evening in time for your driving lessons."

Her smile faltered. "I don't think I can."

"That's part of our deal, Nadia."

A pleat formed between her eyebrows. "Lucas, this is

important and I'm going to be crunched for time. And tonight I have other things to do. I can't drive with you."

"No reneging allowed."

The corners of her mouth turned down. She folded her arms across her chest and lifted her chin. She hit him with a look that probably quelled those who worked beneath her. "You mean like you did on your marriage vows."

Direct hit. Nadia had developed her claws during their time apart. Interesting. *This* was the woman who'd plagued Andvari. She had a new depth that intrigued him far more than she had as a girl of eighteen.

"We both know why our marriage ended. Your father. But admit it. He was probably right. You couldn't have handled being married to a cripple."

She bristled. If she'd been a cat, she'd be hissing. "You don't know that. Like everyone else, you expected me to fail and you didn't give me a chance to prove you wrong." Her lips flattened and she glanced away as if she regretted her outburst.

"You wouldn't have minded doing without sex? I remember you liking that part of our relationship. Very much."

She'd been insatiable. They both had. In fact, it had occurred to him that she hadn't wanted more from him than the stratospheric sex and the chance to flaunt him in her father's face. And then she'd become pregnant.

She sucked in a sharp breath and her eyes widened. Her cheeks pinked. "You couldn't?"

Now he regretted his words. "Not in the first few months. But that wasn't a priority. Walking again was."

"That must have been scary."

Hell, yes. Everything about that whole damned year had scared him. When he'd been told he'd never walk again, his sisters had been sixteen and thirteen, and his mother had already been working two jobs. She'd counted on his salary from Kincaid Manor to make ends meet. He'd seen himself as a burden his family didn't need and couldn't afford. The only way he could make their lives better instead of worse was to take Kincaid's dirty money.

But he wasn't interested in Nadia's psychoanalysis of his decision.

"Dinner's waiting in the oven. Come in. We'll eat before your lesson."

He reached for her satchel, hooking his fingers beneath the leather strap on her shoulder. She resisted giving it up.

"I told you. There's not going to be a lesson tonight. Mitch is getting married at eight eastern time. Rand is arranging for me to see the ceremony via webcam since I can't be there. I'll be in front of my computer tonight."

"Why can't you be there?"

"I just can't. It's too complicated to explain. Even if it wasn't, it's none of your business."

Another puzzle piece from Kincaid's will, he'd bet, like the midnight curfew, her apartment-sitting and the driving instructor she hadn't used. "Come in and eat. I'll make sure you don't miss the wedding."

He lifted her bag again and this time she let him take it. He set it beside the hall table and led the way to his dining room.

Her green eyes swept the table set for two and narrowed on him as he lit the tall white tapers flanking the low bowl of fragrant, floating gardenias. She hung back by the open frosted-glass pocket doors as if looking for an excuse to bolt.

Her gaze probed his. "What are you expecting from me, Lucas? I've told you I'm not interested in resuming our marriage."

"And I'm not willing to write it off without giving it a shot. We had something good, Nadia. Damned good." Although his expectations of happy ever after no longer deluded him.

Sadness clouded her eyes. She shook her head. "I'm not that girl anymore. I can't ever be again."

"Nor am I that kid. But we are still married." He extracted the plates of cracked and cleaned lobsters from the warming oven, scooped servings of new potatoes and caramelized baby carrots onto each dish then carried them to the table. He returned to fetch the drawn butter and bread basket. "Is lobster still your favorite?"

"Yes." Nadia licked her lips but didn't move from the door. "You cooked?"

"Not this time. Be careful of the plate. It's hot." He pulled out her chair, but she didn't move. "Are you still a chocoholic?"

"Yes."

"Then stick around for the molten chocolate lava cake. If we run short on time, we'll eat it in front of your computer or after the wedding. Maybe I can rig your video to play on the TV so you'll have a bigger screen."

With obvious reluctance she crossed the room and took a seat. He retrieved the champagne and popped the cork behind her back. The noise startled her into turning.

She eyed the bottle warily. "What are you celebrating?"

"Finding you again." It should have been a line, a throw-away meaningless phrase. But it didn't feel like one. And the gravel in his voice hadn't been intentional.

Who was he kidding? He *was* glad to have found her and relieved to know she wasn't the selfish bitch he'd believed her to be. Was it wrong to want her to know that he was more than the white trash Everett Kincaid had accused him of being and that he'd multiplied Kincaid's bribe money many times over?

But he wouldn't reveal that data until he absolutely had to—probably when they applied for a new divorce and had to disclose assets. The knowledge of how much this divorce would cost him made him wish he'd signed the prenup Everett Kincaid had tried to force on him. But Nadia had refused and Lucas had supported her decision rather than cave to her father's demands. Back then they'd believed their love and marriage would last forever. Naive of them.

They would divorce. He wasn't going to fall for her again. Love had no place in his life. Besides, unless he wanted to jeopardize the outcome, he couldn't tell her exactly how far he'd come until he'd accomplished his goal of owning KCL. And then she'd want nothing to do with him.

He poured the champagne and joined her at the table. What she'd told him last night had only whet his appetite for details of her life. "You work for KCL. What happened to your plans to turn the New York fashion industry on its head?"

She appeared to give dipping a chunk of lobster into the drawn butter her rapt attention. "My plans changed. I ended up majoring in accounting."

She'd understated her education. According to Terri, Nadia had an MBA and was a CPA with a bunch of other initials after her name. Dry numbers were a far cry from the creativity he remembered. He knew nothing about fashion except what Nadia had told him years ago and what he'd accidentally learned from his sisters. But he'd seen Nadia's portfolio of drawings when they were dating. She'd had talent.

"It's not what you wanted. You had piles of sketch pads full of clothing designs."

"I grew up and realized the chances of me making it in New York were slim to none."

Plausible, but not true—not when you knew the signs. Nadia's eyes didn't lift above his chin and her fingers twitched on the bread. But he'd let her get away with her fib for now. "Why KCL when you didn't get along with your father?"

She chewed and swallowed. "Why not KCL? It's a financially strong company and repeatedly voted one of the best places to work nationwide."

True. And because of KCL's strength and reputation a straight buyout wouldn't be easy. But he'd found a few weaknesses in Kincaid's finances—specifically the billions Everett had borrowed to finance the five new ships he had on order. Lucas was in the process of buying up those loans.

He applied himself to his dinner. Chamberlain's still had the best lobster in Texas. "So he didn't disinherit you for marrying me?"

"No. I guess he changed his mind after he killed you."

A point in the bastard's favor.

"You have to stay in Dallas, can't get a paying job and must be home by midnight. What other hoops does your father have you jumping through?"

She laid aside her lobster fork. "I don't want to talk about him. He's barely been gone two months. And it's…difficult to discuss his last wishes."

The tone of her voice hinted at anger more than grief which only lengthened the list of questions Lucas had about this whole setup. Something wasn't right in this equation and he wouldn't rest until he figured out what was out of kilter.

He wanted to press for details. He needed to know what he was up against. His focus in recent months had been on the Singapore deal and his recon work on KCL had been done before Everett died. The shift in power could alter his strategy.

But he would have to bide his time. Pushing Nadia too hard and too fast for information could alienate her.

If he'd learned nothing else since his accident, it was that his mother's words were true.

Patience was indeed a virtue.

Waiting for the right moment to strike often meant the difference between taking a loss and making the deal of a lifetime.

Nadia found having a man fiddle with her wiring a strangely intimate experience even from thirty feet away. That could be because she couldn't peel her gaze away from the very nice rear end bent over her entertainment cabinet.

"That should do it," Lucas said as he stepped away from her flat panel television. "We should be able to get the webcam feed on the big screen."

"Thank you. But you don't have to stay. I know how much men hate weddings."

"I'll stay in case you have problems with the connection."

As much as she appreciated that, she'd really rather be alone. She didn't expect the next hour to be easy. Weddings never were for her.

But she'd only done one video conference before and the last time Mitch had sent a team of geeks to Dallas to set it up for her. She'd paid attention to the process, but that had been a two-way feed and this was only a one-way deal. It might be different.

The watch-only format left her feeling a little disconnected, but it was better than nothing. She shook off the negative feelings. "How is it you know all this electronic wizardry?"

"I do a lot of my board meetings via video conferencing."

"Why not in person?"

"Like you, I can't always be there." He activated the TV remote then hit a series of keys on her computer—quite competently she noted. Within seconds a jostling image of a candlelit church sanctuary filled the screen.

Her cell phone rang. Caller ID said Rand. "Hi, big brother."

Rand's face entered the picture. "We're live. Check to see if you're getting the audio and video."

He spoke directly into the camera. His voice came through the phone and then, after a slight delay, through the TV speakers. The echoey feel was slightly disorienting.

"I'm getting picture and sound." Her oldest brother looked happier than she'd ever seen him. There was a smile in his eyes.

"I want you to say hello to someone." Rand reached out and wrestled the camera away from the person holding it and then swung it around, leaving Nadia with a room-spinning, carnival ride sensation.

Tara Anthony, a woman who'd been not only Nadia's father's PA but also Nadia's best friend five years ago smiled into the lens. Tara's cheeks were flushed, her blond curls upswept. Rand and Tara's love affair had been another casualty of their father's manipulations and their reunion had come about as a result of his will requiring them to work together. That circumstance had been the main reason Nadia had jumped to the conclusion that her father was trying to reunite her with Lucas.

Wrong.

Tara put Rand's phone to her ear and waved. An engagement ring winked on her finger.

"Hi, Nadia. I wish you were here, but I'll do my best as camera person to make sure you're as close to the action as you can get."

"Thank you." An ache filled Nadia's stomach and rose like a hot-air balloon to block her throat. She wanted to stand beside her brother when he took his vows the way Rand and Mitch had been there for her. "Why didn't Mitch spring for a professional videographer?"

"Your brothers discussed it and decided not to risk a media circus if news of the wedding leaked out. I'm experienced with a camera, so I volunteered."

"Almost showtime," she heard Rand say.

Nadia sank onto the arm of the sofa, her gaze riveted to the screen as Rand panned the camera away from Tara and over the small gathering of guests.

"Nadia, I'm going to hang up now," Tara said into the phone. "We'll talk later. I want to catch up."

"Okay. Bye, Tara." Nadia closed her phone.

An organ struck a chord and blasted through the TV speakers in surround sound. "There's my cue, Rand," Tara said. "Give me the camera. Go stand by your brother and do your best-man thing."

The picture jiggled as Tara took the camera back. Nadia's eyebrows shot up in surprise. Tara had given an order and Rand, second only to their father on the bossy scale, had followed it. Love must indeed have magical powers.

The camera focused on the closed doors at the back of the church. The music swelled and the doors swung open. Seconds later a dark-haired toddler pelted down the aisle as fast as his little arms and legs would churn. He clutched a small white pillow in his fist.

Rhett. Her little brother.

Nadia hurt as if someone had stabbed an ice pick into her chest. She took a jagged breath. Children always had that effect on her, but this one…this one looked enough like her that he could have been hers. She put a fist to her stomach. Her son would have been ten now.

The camera tracked the galloping child to the front of the church then zoomed in on a kneeling, grinning Mitch. Her brother caught the little boy against his chest and hugged him tightly.

"Good job, buddy," she heard Mitch say. Mitch rose with Rhett in his arms, took the pillow with the glistening wedding bands tied on top and passed it to Rand. Then her big, tough, serious older brother planted a kiss on the fuzzy dark head before handing the boy off to a sixtyish woman Nadia didn't recognize.

The next shot framed both of her brothers, Rand standing beside Mitch. Each of them looked happy and relaxed—so different from their forbidding faces at her wedding. Yes, they'd been there to offer support—or pick up the pieces if she'd changed her mind—but they hadn't been cheerful about it. They'd merely been doing their familial duty. Something her father had refused to do.

Mitch's gaze shifted down the aisle. The camera followed and focused on the slender brunette floating toward him with a blinding smile. Carly, Rhett's aunt and soon to be Nadia's sister-in-law. Nadia recognized the lines of the simple ivory Vera Wang dress. Instead of a veil, a ring of flowers intertwined with pearls circled Carly's head. Her face glowed with love, and when the camera panned back to Mitch, the emotion in his expression punched a sob up Nadia's throat.

She was happy for him. Truly, truly happy. But this was something she'd never have.

Love.

Another wedding.

Children.

Her eyes burned. A tear spilled over and burned a path down her cheek. Blinking furiously, she ducked her head and swiped it away, hoping Lucas didn't see. An arm encircled her shoulders. Startled, she looked up. Lucas's blue eyes trained on her face, offering silent support.

They'd once been that happy couple, the one with so much love in their eyes and their hearts that they hadn't seen anyone in the church but each other.

When she looked at him now, she could see remnants of that man and all she could think was, *what a waste* and *how could I have been so wrong about him?*

Lucas had thrown their love away for money. Sure, her father had contributed to the death of their feelings with his meddling, but if Lucas had truly loved her, he would have refused the money. He would have believed in her and her ability to live the vows she'd spoken. In the end, Lucas Stone was the only one to blame for that final blow of the ax.

She shrugged off his arm, hugged her empty, aching middle and fought back a sob. If she'd been alone, she'd probably be crying like a baby.

Her life would have been so different if, in her moment of selfishness, she hadn't distracted him and caused the accident.

Or would it have been?

Would he have betrayed her anyway? But if they hadn't wrecked, even if he'd eventually dumped her, she would have at least had their son and maybe other children for comfort.

Nadia dragged herself out of the well of what-ifs and forced her gaze back to the TV. Tara zoomed in tight on the bride and groom as they took their vows and exchanged rings.

Nadia pressed her trembling lips so tightly together they grew numb. She thumbed her bare ring finger. She'd refused to remove her wedding band for years. Her father had harangued her about it endlessly. The day she'd decided she would never love again, never marry again was the day she'd finally taken off the plain gold band with hers and Lucas's names engraved inside and shoved it into the back of her jewelry armoire.

And that's where it would stay. Forever.

She would never have it all. Never even attempt it. Because she couldn't trust her judgment and she couldn't risk ending up like her mother and hurting or abandoning those who'd loved her. All she could have was her career, her volunteer work and superficial affairs with men she couldn't love.

Men she couldn't love.

The phrase reverberated through her mind like a cry echoing off the Grand Canyon's walls.

Men like Lucas who were more interested in her money than her heart.

Her pulse quickened. Her skin tingled. The fine hairs on her body rose as excitement raced through her.

Her gaze returned to the man beside her. Her husband. The man who had selfishly taken everything precious to her and crushed it. Her chance for happiness. Her love. And more recently, her confidence in her ability to judge others.

Did she dare take what she needed from him? Could she use her soon-to-be ex for mindless physical pleasure and then walk away at the end of her year in exile?

Walk away. Exactly as he'd done to her.

Taboo.

Wrong.

Tempting. Oh, so very tempting.

Seven

"Ready for your chocolate cake and the rest of the champagne?"

Lucas's voice behind her sent a prickle of awareness down Nadia's spine. He'd left her apartment and returned to his immediately after the ceremony ended. Nadia had continued watching as Tara, acting like a TV reporter, led her through the wedding guests to introduce Nadia to Carly, her new sister-in-law, Carly's parents and finally, Rhett, that adorable, beautiful, perfect little boy.

Ignoring the familiar emptiness, Nadia finished shutting down the computer and turned off the TV. She rose and faced Lucas. He carried a tray holding the cake and ice bucket containing the champagne.

Did she dare follow through with her crazy plan?

What do you have to lose? You've already lost everything.

"I don't want dessert or champagne," she told him.

Lucas's eyes narrowed as he closed the distance between them. He set the tray on the coffee table and studied her for several silent seconds. From the day they'd met he'd been able to sense her moods with uncanny accuracy. Neither her father nor her brothers had ever come close to reading her as well as Lucas had. She could tell from his expanding pupils that he'd picked up on her frame of mind this time, too.

"What do you want, Nadia?" His huskier than usual tone said he already knew.

She took a slow, deep breath and ignored the voice in her head urging caution. "You."

"Why?"

She hadn't expected him to make this hard. He never had in the past. She stepped closer, lifted a hand and flattened her palm on his chest. "Because your kisses excite me and your touch enflames me."

And making love with him might fill the emptiness inside. Temporarily. That was all she could ever hope for.

His heart thumped harder and faster beneath her touch and his chest rose on a slowly indrawn breath. His gaze held hers captive as the seconds ticked past. It had never occurred to her that he might refuse. But his lack of action spoke volumes.

She slid her hand upward to cup his nape. The crisp texture of his hair tickled her fingertips and his hot skin warmed her cold fingers. "I want to make love to you, Lucas, like we used to."

His arm banded around her waist, his hand splaying over her lower back. One tug and her body slammed into his. He was hard. Hot. Solid. She could feel each tensed muscle pressed against hers from his thighs through his shoulders. And still he waited. For what?

She wanted mindless passion. Out-of-control lust. She didn't want time to think, to wonder if this was a mistake.

Rising on her tiptoes, she pressed her mouth to his, opened, closed. She sucked his bottom lip between hers. His breath hissed, but he remained tightly leashed unlike in the past when that last maneuver would have made him putty in her hands.

She repeated the kiss with no better results then nibbled her way along his jaw and nipped his earlobe. Eleven years ago a love bite had always brought him to his knees. But not this time. The growing arousal pressing her belly told her he wasn't indifferent. And yet he still didn't capitulate.

Confused by his control when she was rapidly losing hers, she sank back onto her heels.

Lucas's eyes burned like blue fire, which only fanned the flames in her middle. Oh, yeah, he wanted her. So why was he holding back? "We're too old to neck on the sofa. Which bedroom is yours?"

Adrenaline raced through her then caution finally made itself heard. She wanted to scream in frustration. "The one on the left, but I don't have any condoms. Do you? I wasn't expecting…"

With her stupid midnight curfew she hadn't expected to have a nightlife or any kind of life in Dallas.

"My place. Let's go." He released her and bent to lift the tray. Then he walked away.

Taken aback, she blinked after him. *He'd walked away?*

The Lucas she'd known would have taken her anywhere, any way and as often as she'd wanted. It wasn't that he'd been a pushover, but he'd been a young guy, and she'd learned they tended to think with something besides the head on their shoulders. Admittedly, she'd been known to use that fact shamelessly to get what she'd wanted. But the man in question had never complained.

Apparently, the mature Lucas liked to call the shots. That he didn't make the seduction easy ticked her off a little. But it also excited her. And okay, yes, earned her respect. If she wanted him, she'd have to work for it. A wacko part of her relished the challenge.

She followed him out her open door and through his. Tension twined tighter with each step. Or maybe it was arousal. It had been so long since she'd genuinely felt anything remotely resembling lust that she wasn't sure.

She trailed him down his hall, unbuttoning her shirt on the way and draping it over the hall credenza as she passed. She left her shoes with the shirt and reached for the button on her pants. They fell to the floor. A niggle of doubt over what she'd be revealing hitched her step, but she didn't stop. She kicked off the fabric and kept walking.

She'd bet—she hoped—he'd be so distracted by her black sheer demi-bra and panty set when he turned around that he wouldn't be so in control.

And he wouldn't care about the scar. The scar that told the world she was flawed. Imperfect. Incomplete.

He entered a room ahead of her. She followed and paused in the doorway. His bedroom. She surveyed the wide bed with its curved cognac leather headboard and cream-colored spread, then crossed the carpet to stand beside it. A cluster of lush plants created a small jungle near the wall of windows. Outside the uncurtained glass she spotted a patio with more plants, the corner of the swimming pool and the Dallas skyline in the glow of the setting sun.

He deposited his tray on the dresser and turned. His gaze slammed into hers and then slowly rolled over her from head to toe before returning to the scar. She fought the urge to cover it or dive beneath the comforter. It took colossal effort to remain standing and to breathe. That unsightly blemish defined who she was these days. If it turned him off, then that was his problem. She straightened her spine and squared her shoulders.

Without a word his eyes found hers again. He reached for his shirtsleeves and removed the cufflinks, first one, then the other without looking away. The gold clattered noisily on the dark cherry furniture quickly followed by the *thunk* of his watch. With his eyes on hers he continued disrobing, revealing his chest one button at a time.

His shirt fluttered to the floor and she caught her breath. He'd always had a beautiful body, but now he was more muscled, his shoulders wider, his chest deeper, his rippled belly leaner. His hands went to his belt. The chink of the buckle and slither of leather being pulled from the loops seemed unnaturally loud as did the rasp of the zipper. His pants slid down his legs and he kicked them aside. He stood before her in nothing but black silk boxers. The tented front said more than words. Even if he wasn't saying he wanted her, his body was telling her.

What a difference time made. Instead of a lanky twenty-one-year-old boy, Lucas Stone stood in front of her, definitely all man now—every perfect, delicious inch of him.

Her pulse raced and her mouth dried. Her breath grew short as did her patience. What was he waiting for? She reached for the back hook of her bra.

"No."

The quiet but firm command stilled her fingers. Intrigued by this new side of him, she lowered her arms. The old Lucas would have been all over her by now. Any man would. Despite the scar. She had a darned good body and she worked hard to keep in shape. And she only wore the most flattering lingerie.

He prowled toward her. Finally. But instead of yanking her into his arms he pulled back the covers.

Enough stalling.

She wound an arm around his waist and blindly trailed a finger from between his shoulder blades down his spine—the way he'd always loved. Goose bumps lifted his skin in wake of her touch. And then she hit a ridge of flesh at his waist and stopped in surprise. Her gaze jerked to his. He'd said he had surgeries, but somehow she hadn't processed that information.

She grasped his thick biceps and turned him. Her breath hitched. Two straight scars ran parallel to his spine marring his lower back and disappearing beneath his low-riding boxers. She traced the lines with her fingertips tugging the silk over his hips to reveal the paler skin of his butt and the ends of scar tissue. His underwear slid to his ankles and his taut flanks flexed as he kicked them atop his discarded pants.

The lines had faded to silvery-pink, but seeing the damage done by the surgeon's scalpel made her heart ache. They'd both been permanently marked by their accident. In his case, the doctors had given Lucas back his future, his ability to walk and his ability to live a normal life. In hers, they'd taken away the future she'd dreamed of and an ability most women took for granted and sometimes resented. She bent and pressed her lips to the insult on the otherwise perfect V of his tanned back.

A sharply indrawn breath was her only warning before he pivoted, and in one swift strike encircled her waist, yanked her upright and covered her mouth in a hard kiss. The warmth of his body against hers and his silky hot erection against her belly jarred her heart into a rapid rhythm.

Now that's more like it.

But after that initial hard press his kiss wasn't the same. He didn't simply devour her. He sipped, retreated, teased, tempted and tortured her by withholding what she wanted— his tongue in her mouth, his taste, his body deep inside hers. She arched into him, craving his possession, needing to forget. Her present. Her past. Her defects. She needed to feel feminine and desirable.

The rake of his hands from her thighs over her hips and waist to the sides of her breasts went a long way to fulfilling her quest, but still left her wanting more. She dug her nails into his hair and held him while she licked then nipped his bottom lip. He escaped her and transferred his attention to the pulse hammering in her neck. His teeth grazed her skin and the rasp of his evening beard sent a delicious shiver over her. But she wanted to growl in frustration, pound his shoulders and yell faster, faster, more, more, *more*.

She settled for mapping his body, mentally charting the changes in the shape and feel of him. His buttocks clenched under her palms, his tiny nipples tightened beneath her thumbs. His abdominal muscles contracted under her questing fingertips. She loved the texture of his skin, supple and smooth and scorching.

He slid his hands beneath her bikini panties and cupped her bottom, lifting her off her feet and holding her against him. He had her off balance literally and figuratively. She had to clutch his shoulders to maintain her equilibrium.

His lips parted at last. She met the thrust of his tongue with her own. He tasted the same. But everything else had changed. The sure way he caressed and kissed. The make-her-beg-for-it tempo. The hunger. She'd always wanted him. But not like this. This wanting bordered on pain.

The thought jarred her enough to worry her, then she

brushed her concerns away. She hadn't slept with anyone in a long time. Months? A year? Two? She couldn't even remember the last time she'd had sex. She'd been too busy fighting that damned Andvari.

Pent-up passion. That's all this is.

She wound her legs around his waist, cradled his head in her hands and kissed him again and again. Arching and relaxing her back, she rubbed her center against his thick length. Her desire rose swiftly.

Her panties annoyed her. They were in the way. She wanted to be naked, skin to skin and have him buried inside her. Now. Impatient, she tightened her legs and pressed harder against his rigid flesh.

As if he'd received her message, Lucas flicked her bra open. His hands spread over her shoulder blades. He lowered her onto the bed and followed her down, pinning her between the cool sheets and his burning body. Breaking the kiss, he propped on one straight arm long enough to pull the black bra from her and toss it aside, and then he looked at her.

The hunger in his eyes puckered her nipples and tightened her internal muscles. He cupped her breast, thumbed the tip until she gasped and then he bent to take the opposite one into his mouth. The hot, wet swirl of his tongue combined with the magic of his touch made her back bow and her belly contract. And then he tugged with his lips, his teeth and his fingers. A whimper of want escaped her mouth. His caresses robbed her breath, her sanity and her agenda.

She couldn't remember the last time a man's touch had felt this good. A molten sensation invaded her muscles. She tunneled her fingers into his hair and held him, silently pleading for more. But he abandoned her breasts.

His lips traveled lower. He nuzzled the sensitive undersides before drifting with featherlight whispers across her ribs and then toward her navel. The haze of hunger morphed into a clear chill of tension when she realized where he was headed. She fisted her fingers in his hair and tugged. When that didn't work she dug her heels into the mattress and tried to twist away, but he easily pinned her down.

"Lucas, don't."

"We all have scars, Nadia. Some show. Some don't." His tongue swept down the length of the rippled flesh from her navel to her panties and then back up again to swirl in her belly button.

The move should have repelled her. She hated that scar. Hated what it represented. She never let anyone touch it. Instead, her breath hitched and strangely, she couldn't seem to gather the strength to shove him off. And then he pressed his mouth to her lacy bikinis and his breath steamed right through the thin fabric exactly where she needed his touch the most.

Thoughts of pushing him away vanished under the on-slaught of prurience. She quit struggling and savored the sensation of his chin circling over her flesh with the perfect amount of pressure, the perfect tempo. His fingers edged beneath her elastic leg band at her hip and drifted down toward her center, then away and back again. She groaned and squirmed. He delved deeper, finding her moisture and massaging it in with exquisite thoroughness.

She climbed swiftly. She wanted to whisper words of encouragement, but she couldn't seem to string the phrases together to make her request. All she could do was clutch his hair, the sheets, lift her hips toward his mouth. Release gathered. He eased away from her seconds before she went over the edge. And then he did it again, and again, caressing, arousing and retreating until she thought she'd scream.

"Lucas, please."

He planted a lingering kiss on her hipbone then rolled away and opened a drawer. While he donned the condom she shimmied out of her panties and then lay back, propped on her elbows with one knee bent in what she hoped he'd find an irresistible, inviting pose.

He returned to her, but instead of moving over her and giving her the sexual oblivion she needed, he skimmed her curves with his fingertips, circling each nipple, outlining her waist, her navel and her triangle of curls. Aching and growing more desperate by the second from his teasing sensuality, she writhed beneath him and tried to rise, planning to drag him back down with her. Lucas planted two fingers on her breastbone and pushed her back down gently, but firmly. The commanding look in his eyes warned her not to argue.

A thrill shot through her. She wasn't used to this man who wouldn't be led or coerced.

Without breaking eye contact he leaned over and kissed her bent knee, then the inside of her thigh. His lips lifted and touched down, each time landing closer to her center, each time making her gasp with a lick or a nip or the rasp of his chin. The prickle of his evening beard on her tender skin excited her unbearably. Her breathing shallowed, quickened, until she was nearly panting. And he knew it. He knew because he watched and noted every hiccup of breath, every quiver, every time she had to bite her lip to keep from crying out.

As if they'd been together like this just yesterday instead of more than a decade ago, he found her pleasure points with unerring accuracy. His tongue flicked over exactly the right spot and orgasm crashed over her with shocking speed. Her eyes slammed shut. His name poured from her lips and her body jerked as her muscles clenched and released over and over.

When the last erotic spasm died he rose to his hands and knees and prowled up her body until he poised above her, his eyes dark with passion and intent. His elbows bent. He took her mouth in a kiss so carnal, so hot and wet and decadent and delicious she could only cling to him. Their tongues tangled and dueled. Their lips alternated between butterfly soft and branding hot. She couldn't get enough of him, of this new version of him.

His fingertips found her entrance, stroked, readied her, and then his blunt tip took their place. She held her breath and waited for him to fill her. And then he did. Languorously. She dug her nails into his buttocks and urged him to hurry, but he wouldn't be rushed. Each long, slow glide in and out filled her with an impatient craving for more.

She lifted her hips, meeting each thrust, and when he released her mouth to suck a sharp breath, she watched his eyes darken as hunger gave them a common goal. She arched upward to nip his shoulder, his neck. His scent filled her nostrils; the slightly salty taste of him pervaded her mouth and his deep thrusts filled her body. Her palms skimmed his back, his buttocks, his waist and chest. The scrape of her nails on his neck made him shudder against her.

She relished the crack in his control. And yet he still didn't speak. The Lucas of her past had been verbal. He'd told her how good she tasted, how good she felt, how hot she made him and how much he loved her. Especially the last one. And she'd been so hungry for those words. Yet despite his silence, his eyes said it all.

For the first time in forever she could feel every sensitized inch of her skin, particularly the parts melding to the heat of his or abraded by the coarse hair on his legs. She felt alive and wanted and desirable and womanly instead of flawed. She banished the sobering thought and focused on the stroke of his hand where they were joined and relished the depth of his penetration.

He filled her, surrounded her, energized her. Her climax built anew, tightening her muscles, stealing her breath, muddling her thoughts. And then it hit. Hard. Fast. Consuming her completely. Sapped, she lay enervated beneath him, so weakened her hands could barely cling to his waist.

His thrusts deepened, quickened and then his groan of completion filled her ears as he shuddered above her. Seconds later muscles went lax and his weight settled on her.

He braced himself above her so that he didn't crush her, but with each of their gasped breaths her breasts kissed his chest.

Making love with Lucas hadn't remotely resembled the mindless sex she'd used in the past to help her forget. No. Making love with him felt good and right.

But was it a mistake?

Did she dare give him a second chance to turn her world upside down?

Eight

*T*oo good.

Are you nuts, man? How in the hell can anyone complain about sex being too good?

Lucas rolled away from Nadia, needing to put both mental and physical distance between them. He had an agenda and he had to stick to it. He couldn't allow making love with Nadia to cloud the issue.

He retreated to the bathroom, disposed of the condom and splashed cold water on his face. He had what he wanted. His wife in his bed. Trusting him. Open to him. A little more persuasion and she'd answer whatever questions he asked, enabling him to get an insider's view on KCL's weaknesses and plan the best attack route.

But getting lost in Nadia's scent, the softness of her skin, the wet heat of her body and her brain-twisting kisses didn't feel like work. It felt good. Too damned good.

No such thing.

Get your head back in the game.

He pushed away from the vanity, pulled on his robe and returned to the bedroom. Nadia, wearing his shirt, sat with her back against the center of the headboard, her long, gorgeous legs bent, ankles tucked beneath her. Her gaze followed him as he crossed to the dresser and retrieved the tray holding the cake and chilling champagne. He joined her on the bed, placing the tray on the mattress between them.

He filled the champagne flutes and offered her one. "Ready for dessert? Sex always gave you an appetite."

She fumbled the glass, nearly dropping it, and averted her face. Was she blushing? Had he ever seen Nadia blush? No. She'd always been bold and aggressive, sure of what she wanted and her entitlement to it. Her take-no-prisoners attitude had been a real turn-on.

But so was this unexpectedly shy side.

"I guess some things never change." Her eyes didn't quite meet his as she picked up a fork, cut into the lava cake and put the small wedge into her mouth.

A crumb clung to her bottom lip. He stifled the urge to lap it up and ate a forkful of the moist chocolaty confection. The rich flavor filled his mouth, erasing what was left of Nadia's taste he noted with a disgustingly sappy hint of regret. He washed it down with a gulp of champagne.

She looked up at him through her lashes. "Why did you take the money, Lucas?"

He sucked in a sharp breath and almost choked on the bubbly beverage. What the hell. What would it hurt to tell her?

"Because I was afraid I'd be a burden to my family. Your father made sure I knew exactly how much debt I was racking up with each day I stayed in the hospital. I was looking at months more of hospital time plus the surgeries. I knew I couldn't afford any of it since I lost my health insurance when your father fired me and the policy from my new job hadn't kicked in yet. But staying for treatment was my only chance to ever walk again.

"My mother and I were barely making ends meet with our combined salaries, and it looked like I'd be unable to work for a long time. Your father's bribe guaranteed we'd keep a roof over our heads and that my sisters would get a good education—something I was no longer sure I could provide."

Nadia's breath shuddered in and then out. Understanding softened her eyes and mouth. "I should have known you weren't thinking of yourself. You always put your family first. Your girls, you called them."

For a brief few months she'd been one of his "girls," and she'd always beamed when he'd told her that.

"Your brothers would do the same for you." A point in Rand and Mitch's favor.

"Yes. They would. That's why I can't let them down this time. There's too much at stake. I have to get it right."

He topped off her glass and then nodded toward her middle. "What happened, Nadia?"

Her sudden stillness told him she knew what he meant. She toyed with the dessert, cut a wedge and mashed it between the tines of her fork, but she didn't eat it. The silence stretched so long he didn't think she'd answer.

"I lost our son and the ability to have other children. They had to take my uterus to stop the bleeding."

Their son. He'd often wondered.

The ache in his chest ambushed him from out of nowhere. Grief? Too late for that. He never wasted energy or emotion on anything he couldn't change.

Before the wedding he and Nadia had discussed having children. A lot of them. They'd both wanted a large family. Nadia had wanted their kids to be close in age so they'd have each other as playmates—something she hadn't had with her brothers who'd been four and six years older. It had been the same for him with Sandi and Terri. Their gender and age differences had kept them from being close.

After Kincaid had fired Lucas for refusing to break it off with Nadia, the bastard had made sure Lucas couldn't get a job with anyone else in the Kincaid's exalted Miami circle. Lucas had finally found a new job with a different landscaping company. The pay hadn't been nearly as good as working for the Kincaids, but there had been room for advancement.

He hadn't known how he was going to support a wife let alone children and help his family, but he'd figured they'd find a way. His mother always had.

"I'm sorry we lost our son." The words sounded as empty as he felt.

She shrugged as if it didn't matter but the tears she blinked away told him it mattered a lot. Then she knocked back half her glass of champagne in one gulp. "I could have had plastic surgery to minimize the scar, but what's the point? They can't put back what they took."

Not even a moron could miss the point that the scar wasn't the issue. He wanted to know the details, but unless things had changed over the years, when Nadia wore that closed expression she wasn't going to talk. He'd have to tease the information out of her slowly or risk closing the door their intimacy had opened. And that open door was critical to his plan.

He decided to try a different path. "Is that why you never married again? Because you couldn't have children?"

"What was the point? No family. No need for a ring. But, no. I didn't marry because I found out after my—our wreck— that my mother was mentally unstable. Her accident was intentional. She drove Daddy's prized sports car straight into a tree and killed herself rather than stay at home and take care of the ones who needed her."

Shock chilled him. "What do you mean she was mentally unstable?"

"My mother was manic depressive or bipolar, if you want to use the most up-to-date term. It's believed to be hereditary, you know? And while the legion of shrinks my father sicced on me over the years swears I don't carry her defective gene, they can't be one hundred percent sure. I'll never marry, never adopt children, and never let anyone depend on me. It's a risk I don't want to take."

The news settled over him, making sense of the crazy stories he'd read about Nadia in the tabloids over the years. She lived as though she had nothing to lose. Because she believed she didn't?

She shifted on the bed, flashing him a glimpse of inner thigh and stirring the scent of their lovemaking in the air. Arousal kicked him hard in the gut. He wanted her again, wanted to saturate himself in her until there were no crevices of need left to fill. And then he'd let her go.

But duty called. He had to leave her in thirty-six hours. Unless... "Come to Singapore with me."

Her chin jerked up. "What?"

"I have to be in Singapore first thing Monday morning to close a deal. The CEO handling the deal I'm closing is a sexist jerk. He refuses to talk to Sandi."

Nadia bit her lip and looked into her glass. "I can't."

"You can work on the fund-raiser from your laptop."

Her gaze met his. She opened her mouth as if to say something, then closed it again. Grimacing, she downed the remainder of her champagne then took a deep breath. "I can't leave Dallas because of my father's stupid will. I have to spend 365 consecutive nights in Daddy's penthouse."

The restriction explained the anger he'd heard in her voice each time she'd spoken about her father. Everett Kincaid had always held too tightly to his baby girl. Eleven years ago Lucas had known that was a mistake and had tried to warn Kincaid he'd lose Nadia if he didn't loosen his grip. That's when Kincaid had fired him.

"And if you don't?"

"I told you before. We lose our inheritance. Daddy gave each of us an assigned task. If any one of us fails, then everything—and I do mean *everything* he owned—will be sold to his enemy for a dollar. Mitch and Rand are well on their way to fulfilling their part. I'm the wild card, the one everyone expects to fall short. That's why I can't mess this up. They're counting on me."

That KCL could be sold out from under him jarred him. He hadn't seen that coming. "His enemy?"

"What kind of father screws his own children like that?" she asked, ignoring his question.

A father like mine. But he didn't say it. He'd never told Nadia about the good-for-nothing bastard who'd knocked up Lila Stone, married her without mentioning he already had a wife and kids then dumped his wife and son without a backward glance. He'd told Nadia his father was gone, and when she'd assumed he meant dead, Lucas hadn't corrected her.

She stabbed the fork into the cake and ate another bite. "I mean it's ridiculous. He took away my job—the one thing I'm good at—and he forced me to give up my friends and my home.

He gave me a curfew and an allowance and took away my maid, cook and driver. He's treating me like a misbehaving thirteen-year-old by grounding me and taking away privileges."

"It's a bit harsh." But not surprising. Dogmatic decrees had been Everett Kincaid's style. The man had been an extreme control freak. It's a wonder any of his children had remained on speaking terms with him. "Who is his enemy?"

She stared at him, blinked and then she smiled and reached for him. Her palm cupped his jaw line. "Let's not talk about my idiot father. Let's make love again. I adore the way you make me feel, Lucas. You help me forget all this crazy will business."

Her hand slid down his neck and over his collarbone, inciting a riot of sensation and short-circuiting his brain. The last thing he wanted to do was lift her wandering fingers from his chest, but he did because there was no way he could focus on his agenda with her touching him. And he needed to know who stood between him and ownership of KCL.

He kissed her fingers, then couldn't resist swirling his tongue around the tips. Her flavor filled his mouth and left him craving more, but he ignored the hunger clawing his insides and settling heavily in his groin. Why was it that no other woman had affected him this way? "If you can't go with me, then give me until Sunday night."

"But the fund-raiser—"

"What did you decide to do about it?" he asked in an attempt to rein in his need.

"We'll have an auction. I need to nail down the prizes this week and get the promotional materials released."

"If you'll spend Saturday and Sunday with me, I'll give you a list of firms and individuals in the Dallas area who will donate."

She tilted her head, giving him a look that started out

curious then turned saucier by the second. "You're sure you can deliver the goods?"

A fresh wave of arousal slammed into his gut. She wasn't just talking about prizes. "Absolutely. I can give you whatever you need."

One corner of her delectable mouth curved upward and sexual mischief sparkled in her green eyes. "I'll hold you to that. I'll bet I can get Rand and Mitch to donate a cruise… assuming the business is still ours when the time comes for the winner to take it."

Which dampened his desire and brought him neatly back to the subject burning a hole in his brain. "I'm sure your father had numerous enemies, but who would he leave his estate to?"

She sighed and pulled away, a sound of disgust rumbling from her throat. "Mardi Gras Cruising."

Shock winded him. He was glad she had her back to him long enough for him to gather his composure. Dozens of thoughts avalanched through his mind. Primarily, the terms of Kincaid's will added to the purchase of the apartment could only mean one thing. Everett Kincaid must have been tracking him all these years. But how? And why?

Lucas was a firm believer in knowing his enemies as well as possible. Had Kincaid practiced the same philosophy? Or was it something more?

He had to find out. "Why Mardi Gras?"

She turned, rolling her eyes. "I don't know. Dad absolutely detested the CEO. They've had a running battle for years because Mardi Gras kept encroaching on our turf by under-bidding us on an assortment of contracts. It really seemed to get under Dad's skin. I can't believe he would rather see the Mardi Gras logo on our ships than have Rand, Mitch and I continue the KCL tradition of running an award-winning organization."

Lucas was well aware Mardi Gras's CEO was an aggressive, cutthroat ass who stayed just this side of legal in his pursuits. That's why he'd hired him. The man was as determined and focused on besting the competition as Lucas. And he was power-hungry. That meant he wasn't about to let slip that many of his decisions came as direct orders from his behind-the-scenes boss.

And then another thought hit Lucas with chilling clarity.

KCL could be his.

All he had to do was get Nadia to leave Dallas.

He weighed the knowledge. But would winning by default give him half the satisfaction as taking KCL by stealth and skill?

And would it be revenge if what he wanted was handed to him by the very man who'd taught him the meaning of defeat?

"Nadia, wake up," a deep voice repeated more urgently this time. Lucas's voice.

Nadia smiled and snuggled deeper into the warmth cocooning her. She fully intended to ignore whoever was trying to rouse her from a dream she hadn't had in almost five years. A dream of Lucas holding her, making love to her. She'd missed that dream.

"Go 'way."

"It's almost midnight."

"Don't care," she mumbled. She knew from experience that when she opened her eyes that would not be Lucas in her bedroom. No matter how much it sounded like him now.

The pillow beneath her shifted, dumping her as it rose. *Pillows rising?* Her fogged brain slowly cleared. She reached out blindly in the darkness. Her fingers encountered supple skin covering a taut backside instead of Egyptian cotton and down.

Oh, man. Who had she slept with this time? Another poor sap who reminded her of her dead husband?

But she hadn't done a Lucas look-alike in…a long time.

And Lucas wasn't dead.

Startled, she popped upright. The lamp clicked on. She winced and shielded her eyes, but not before catching a glimpse of her naked husband beside the bed stepping into his pants. Her body tingled at the memory of how they'd passed the preceding hours.

"Get up. You have to get back to your place."

Her place. *Midnight.* Panic erased the last remnants of grogginess from her brain. She leaped from the bed and scanned the floor. "My clothes. I don't know where I left—"

"You don't have time for your clothes. There are security cameras in the hall. Put this on." He held out his robe.

She checked his clock as she shoved her arms into the black silk sleeves then cinched the belt. Two minutes to midnight. She'd nearly blown it. Her father was right. She truly did need a keeper, and she'd have to be more careful in the future. "I can't believe I almost messed up. Thank you for waking me."

He wore an odd expression on his face, one she didn't have time to decipher.

"C'mon." He grabbed her elbow and hauled her through his apartment, his stride rapid and almost angry. She hustled to keep up, snatching discarded clothing as she raced for the door.

They blasted across the hall and through her unlocked door just as the clock started chiming. She blew out a breath. "We made it, but that was too close for comfort. Coming in?"

She hoped he would. Making love with Lucas had been even better than she remembered. She wasn't sure if that would come back to haunt her, but she'd never know if she didn't pursue this.

Lucas didn't look the least bit interested in round three. He looked tense and maybe even pissed off.

What did he have to be angry about? "Lucas, what's wrong?"

"Good night, Nadia."

She hooked his elbow as he turned away. "The will says I can't host parties. It doesn't say I can't have an overnight guest."

A nerve twitched in his jaw. "Get some sleep. I'll give you an early morning driving lesson and then we'll tour some of the local gardens."

"But—"

He latched his hand around her nape and pulled her forward for a hard and fast kiss. The smooch ended before she could react. "I'll see you in the morning."

He turned away, reentered his apartment and shut the door. The lock clicked.

She sank back on her heels. Well, that had never happened before.

Men didn't throw her out. Was this only a prelude to what she could expect from him in the future? Because she really didn't like the way it made her feel. And that was a bitter pill to swallow because she'd done the same thing too many times to count while trying to forget her dead—her husband.

She'd used men for a few minutes of oblivion, to feel complete and whole, then she'd dumped them. Suddenly, she didn't like the person she'd become very much. Using people was one bad habit she'd have to break.

* * *

"Close your eyes."

Nadia lifted her gaze from the beautiful lily to Lucas's face. "Why?"

"Just do it."

He hadn't been so bossy before. And in the past she would have told him exactly what he could do with that attitude, but learning to deal with her father over the years had made her slightly less prickly.

He shoved his Oakley sunglasses up into his golden hair, revealing the blue eyes she'd fallen head over heels for more than a decade ago—eyes she was in danger of drowning in again today. "You claim you've learned to cook. Let's see how good you are at identifying your ingredients."

He withdrew a white handkerchief from his back jeans pocket and folded it first into a triangle and then into a band which he stretched between his hands.

Her pulse kicked erratically and her mouth dried. "Are you making a blindfold?"

"Yes."

They'd never done kinky sex before, and she wasn't expecting to start now on a Saturday afternoon in the Texas Discovery Gardens with other guests and even children around. On the other hand, if he took her back to the penthouse she'd be more than willing to play whatever games he dished out.

Making love with him last night had made her feel whole for the first time in a long time. She wanted more even though that meant opening herself up for more pain and disappointment, and she'd become very protective of her wounded heart over the years.

"The scent garden behind you was originally developed

for the blind." She started to turn and look, but he caught her elbow and held her in place. "No cheating."

Eleven years ago Lucas had shown her a side of life she never would have experienced inside the Kincaid compound walls. And she'd loved it. She decided to cut him some slack today. They were in a public place. How could it go wrong? "Okay, fine, but no blindfold."

"Don't you trust me, Nadia?"

The multibillion dollar question. Could she ever trust Lucas Stone again? She didn't have the answer. Yet. Yes, she understood his reasons for taking the money. But he'd left her alone to grieve. He couldn't possibly know how close she'd come to— She cut off the thought. She wasn't that wounded woman anymore. She'd come a long way and made a success of her life.

"Fine. Do it."

He stepped behind her. The white fabric fluttered over her head coming to rest over her eyes and the bridge of her nose. His fingers teased her hair as he tied the ends in the back. Goose bumps rose on her arms despite the heat of the day. He might not intend this to be an arousing experience, but the sizzle percolating through her veins was definitely sexual.

Without her sight her senses suddenly seemed sharper. She could feel the warmth radiating off his body, smell the lilies in front of her and the man behind her. She leaned against him, letting him blanket her body with heat. His arms tightened around her waist. His cologne combined with his natural muskiness caused by their hour-long stroll through the gardens on this hot August day filled her nostrils. She licked her lips and tilted her head against his shoulder wanting his taste.

He squeezed her waist then his breath steamed the underside of her jaw a split second before his lips touched down on the pulse quickening in her neck. "Ready?"

For more than blindly sniffing plants. "Sure."

"Good." He gripped her shoulders then turned her around and urged her forward for several yards. His grip tightened, stopping her. His fingertips stroked down her bare arm, arousing a shiver from her. He caught her hand and scraped his nails lightly over her palm then guided her fingers over the pointy leaves of a plant before carrying her hand to her nose.

"Tell me what you smell."

She inhaled. "Rosemary."

"Good. But that was an easy one."

He urged her forward. His tightening grip stopped her after five steps. This time he stroked the tender flesh inside her opposite arm. Desire simmered inside her. His fingers threaded through hers, his palm flattening over the back of her hand, and then he brushed their joined hands over a smooth, cool plant. Together they lifted her hand to her nose.

She inhaled and smelled him and… "Mint."

"Very good." His lips brushed her ear as he whispered the words. His teeth grazed her lobe.

She nearly moaned, but because of the blindfold she didn't know who was around and didn't dare. And just like making love in the church anteroom after their wedding, the idea of getting caught intensified her reaction and filled her with a naughty thrill.

His hips nudged hers forward. She could feel his growing length pressing against her lower back telling her he wasn't unaffected by their little game.

He stopped her again, but instead of gripping her hand, this time his fingers curled around her waist and glided upward.

Under the cover of her arms his thumbs brushed the sides of her breasts. Her breath hitched.

"Reach out and to your left," he ordered in a gravelly tone. His fingers grazed the underside of her breasts stirring an ache low in her belly. "A little more."

Her thoughts exactly. He was only inches from touching her tight nipple. It took every ounce of restraint not to turn in his arms and press her flesh into his palm. Her fingers encountered leaves. She fondled the plant, stroking the fronds the way she wanted to stroke Lucas's skin.

His breath tickled her ear. "What do you smell?"

Him. She smelled him. And sunlight and flowers and she searched her memory to identify the herb. "Thyme."

He grip tightened then released. Her skin cooled without his touch. And then a warm palm cradled her jaw, angled her head and his lips covered hers as softly as a butterfly touching down.

He peeled the blindfold from her eyes. "You have two choices. We can finish the garden tour and go on to the aquarium. Or we can go back to the apartment."

The passion burning in his eyes made her breath hitch. She was falling for him again. Making love with him now would be as good as surrendering to those feelings.

Did she dare risk it?

Did she even have a choice?

He lifted her knuckles to his lips and her stomach somersaulted. No. She didn't have a choice. Because as much as she wanted to hate Lucas for leaving her, she was afraid she was still very much in love with him.

Nine

The black Lincoln limo gleaming beneath a streetlight tempted Nadia more than chocolate when she stepped out of the library late Monday night.

Old habits died hard.

She glanced at her watch, disgusted with herself because she'd lost track of time and stayed later than she should have. But she hadn't wanted to go back to the apartment, which felt emptier now that Lucas had left the building.

She'd have to splurge for a taxi. Once upon a time she would have done so without a second thought. Now it meant she'd have to cut something else out of her budget.

She glared up at the cloud-dotted sky. *Yes, Daddy, I am learning to identify with our largest demographic.*

Turning down the sidewalk, she scanned the streets which were disgustingly empty. It was Monday night. Not much going on in this section of downtown.

"Ms. Kincaid?"

She pivoted quickly. A swarthy man—thirtyish and muscular—in a chauffeur's uniform walked toward her. Years of ingrained caution kicked in. She might choose to live a relatively normal life without bodyguards, but she was still worth billions and kidnapping was a real possibility. Her father had harped on it endlessly—especially after that close call when she was twelve.

Why don't you carry pepper spray like a normal twenty-nine-year-old woman?

"Stop right there," she shouted.

The guy held up both hands and halted three yards away. "I'm Paulo. Mr. Stone asked me to provide your transportation while he's away."

Right. She hadn't been born yesterday. She wasn't getting into a strange car with darkly tinted windows just because the guy knew Lucas's name.

"I don't need a ride. Thank you." She backed toward the library. The doors were locked. Mary, the head librarian, had locked them after letting Nadia out. But she could hammer on the glass and scream until Mary or somebody heard her. And if they didn't come Nadia could run around back to the employee parking lot and hope she could catch Mary before she left. Of course, Nadia would have to leave her Christian Louboutin sandals behind if she wanted to sprint. But thousand-dollar shoes were a small price to pay for safety.

"He said you'd probably refuse and that I should call him if you did." He reached into his pocket and she prepared herself to kick off her shoes and run, but he didn't withdraw a weapon. He held a phone—a six-hundred-dollar phone. She recognized the brand because she owned one just like it. Extending his arm, he walked toward her.

"Stop," she repeated and dug her cell phone out of her bag. She'd call the police if he didn't go away.

"Yes, ma'am. I'll just dial Mr. Stone and put him on speaker for you."

He punched in a series of numbers. She called herself all kinds of fool for not running while he was preoccupied, but his suit was of good quality and it fit as if the limo company had tailored it for him. Only the top-notch places did that. Maybe Lucas had hired a car for her. The idea gave her the warm fuzzies.

"Did you find her?" Lucas's voice said over the speaker and her stomach fluttered.

"Yes, sir. I have Ms. Kincaid here and she reacted exactly as you predicted. We're on speaker phone. Maybe you could tell her I'm legit?"

"Nadia, can you hear me?"

"Yes." She pitched her voice to carry across the distance.

Lucas had been gone less than twenty-four hours and she wanted to talk to him, to tell him about her day and the fund-raising plans. The list of potential contributors he'd given her combined with the names she'd gathered on her own and a day's worth of phone time had garnered more donations than she'd ever hoped for. This fund-raiser could be the best in library history.

"Paulo is at your disposal while I'm gone. I don't want you taking the train."

Part of her was pleased that he'd thought of her. Another teensy part pricked her pride because he'd assumed she would do something foolish. "I'm not dumb enough to ride alone this late at night. I was going to take a taxi."

"Now you don't have to."

She considered arguing. After all, she was trying to stand

on her own two feet and prove she could. Relying on Lucas was no better than relying on Mitch or Rand or her father. But refusing for the sake of principal would be beyond stupid.

"I'll worry less if you use the car especially coming home from the library after dark," Lucas said as if he could read her mind.

Something inside her melted. Lucas was trying to take care of her. He'd done that eleven years ago, too. "You could have told me you were hiring a driver."

"Paulo, turn off the speaker and give Ms. Kincaid the phone, please."

Paulo did as ordered.

Nadia pressed the phone to her ear. "I'm here."

"You had me otherwise occupied before I left and I neglected to get your cell number."

His intimate pitch sent her pulse stuttering irregularly. Her skin warmed even more than the balmy summer night warranted when she recalled exactly how he'd been occupied. He'd spent Saturday night and most of Sunday in her bed. Exploring every inch of her skin and letting her relearn his.

"Thanks for thinking of me, Lucas."

Paulo opened the back door of the limo and she climbed in. The supple leather seats cradled her, a nice change after a long day in the hard, inexpensive office chair the library had found for her to use.

"We made a mess of your place. I've asked Ella to come over and clean up."

Her stomach did another flip. They'd wrecked her bed and then her kitchen when midnight cooking in the nude had turned into sex on the table complete with whipped cream, raspberry jam and chocolate sauce.

Her skin flushed. "I've already cleaned up. But thank you."

"You're sure?"

"I'm sure. My father didn't think I could manage the real-world chores of cooking and cleaning up after myself. I like proving him wrong." Crazier still, she liked seeing the place gleam and knowing it was due to her efforts.

"Everett always underestimated you."

"I know. I'm so much more than just a pretty face." She said the words tongue in cheek and he rewarded her with a chuckle.

"Yes, you are. Think of me when you go to bed tonight."

The low timber of his voice sent a shiver of arousal over her. She angled away from Paulo as he slid into the driver's seat. "I think it's safe to say I'll be doing that."

"And what will you be doing while you're thinking of me?"

Heat rushed through her and pooled low in her belly. "Remembering."

"Will you touch yourself the way I did?"

She struggled to pull a calming breath into her suddenly tight chest. "That's for me to know and you to wonder."

He tsked. "Trust me. I will. I'll see you in a few days and get the details of how you filled your nights. Good night, Nadia."

The call ended abruptly. Disappointed, she stared at the phone, then she composed herself and passed it through the open partition to Paulo. "Thanks."

"Would you like to go home? Or do you need to stop somewhere else first?"

"No. I want to go home. I mean, to the apartment."

And for the first time that was the truth. She'd had an amazing night followed by an even more amazing few days, and she couldn't wait to climb into a tub and savor how much her life had changed. And she wanted to go to sleep on the pillow case she hadn't washed—the one that smelled of Lucas.

Funny. Being stuck in Dallas didn't feel like a death sentence anymore. She hoped that in this case history wasn't about to repeat itself. Because she wasn't sure she'd survive losing him a second time.

Nadia's cell phone vibrated in her pocket Friday morning. *Lucas?*

She snatched it out and angled her back to the door of the tiny office Mary had assigned to her. But the caller ID said Rand instead of Lucas.

"Hi, big brother." She hoped he didn't hear the disappointment in her voice, but his wasn't the baritone she wanted to hear. "Did Mitch's wedding give you and Tara any ideas?"

"Don't worry. When we set a date, you'll be the first to know. I'm not going to let Tara get away this time. Nadia, what can you tell me about Andvari, Inc.?"

He sounded tense. "Why?"

"Because Teckitron, an Andvari subsidiary, just bought up the loans Dad took out to finance the new ships he has on order."

She jerked in surprise. "Why would he have taken out loans? We had the capital. Didn't we?"

"Mitch says Dad had some grand theory about saving money by writing off the finance charges on KCL's taxes and he wouldn't listen to reason. You know how he was when he got an idea. And remember Dad dumped a huge chunk of our ready cash into refurbishing the ships and some of that cash was mismanaged. Mitch and I are still unraveling that mess and auditing the other lines to make sure there isn't more embezzling going on than we already know about. I need everything you can tell me about Andvari."

"Sounds urgent."

"I want to find out who's behind that company. When you add Andvari buying up our suppliers over the past few years to the recent purchase of the bank holding our loans the situation begins to look like more than a coincidence."

"What do you mean?"

"I mean someone has it in for KCL. A personal vendetta. Not surprising since Dad managed to make a few enemies."

She flinched. Rand had never been prone to paranoia or jumping to conclusions. If he was worried, then he had grounds.

Daddy, what have you done?

"I have an Andvari file on my computer. It's woefully incomplete because I just haven't been able to penetrate the Andvari bureaucracy. I'll tell my assistant to e-mail it to you. But good luck with your research. What kind of hole does this leave us in, Rand? Worst-case scenario, if this Teckitron calls the loans we can pay them back. Right?"

The tense silence made the hairs on her body rise. "Given enough time we should be able to raise the capital. But because of the terms of the will we're in an awkward spot financially. Everything's tied up. We can't liquidate any assets or investments.

"To a new creditor we're a high-risk venture because any one of us could blow this thing right out of the water by violating one part of the damned inheritance curse. If that happens, all Kincaid properties are gone and we have no collateral. No one is going to risk billions without collateral.

"God help us when the terms of his will are made public.

The press is going to have a field day. The media furor has barely died down surrounding Dad's death. If the loans being bought up leaks, it'll stir up the hornet's nest again."

Not good. "Get our PR team on it. Have them prepare a statement. If anyone can spin this in a positive direction, they can."

"I'll do it." He paused and the awkward silence had her bracing herself in her stiff-backed chair. "How are you? And what's going on with Stone?"

She raked her hair back from her face and decided to come clean. "I'm in love with him again."

"Nadia—"

"Don't Nadia me. Lucas was as much a victim of Dad's machinations as you and Tara were. Dad was wrong to break you up. Well, he was wrong to break Lucas and me up, too."

"There's a difference. Tara refused Dad's bribe money."

Yes, okay, there was that. Their father had offered Tara an obscene amount of money to be his mistress. She'd not only refused, but also she'd quit her prestigious job as Everett Kincaid's PA and left the company and her friends—including Nadia—behind.

Nadia would be lying if she didn't acknowledge it bothered her that Lucas hadn't been as noble. "He had good reasons for taking the cash."

"Don't wear blinders, Nadia. If he betrayed you once, he'll do it again."

Her stomach churned. "I don't think he will."

"For your sake, I hope you're right. But whatever happens, I've got your back."

A chime sounded announcing an instant message on Nadia's computer an hour after her disturbing phone call from her brother.

Dreading more bad news from Rand, she reluctantly put down the impressive list of prizes she'd accumulated for the library fund-raiser and swiveled the laptop to face her.

LDStone: Working?

Her pulse skipped when she saw the name in the message box at the top left corner of her screen.

Lucas Daniel Stone. She'd named their son after his daddy and called him Daniel. Her eyes burned and her hands trembled as she poised them over the keyboard.

NEKincaid: Yes. How did you get my Messenger ID?

LDStone: I have my ways. And I'd like to show them to you. Preferably in bed. Naked.

Her insides bunched into a hot, smoldering knot of need. He'd been gone a week. A week during which he'd phoned at least once a day and told her in explicit detail what he would be doing to her if he were in Dallas instead of on the opposite side of the globe. This new aggressive side of him turned her on like crazy. It was like having the old Lucas back in a new and improved version. And without the headache of battling her father over him.

LDStone: I'll be home tonight. I'll wear the blindfold this time.

Her breath caught. She plucked at her suddenly sticking Juicy Couture shirt. They'd made use of that blindfold Saturday night and her skin tingled anew at the remembered blind anticipation of his touch.

NEKincaid: I can't wait. She frowned. But I'll probably be late. I'm supposed to meet with the committee tonight to give them a status update. They're a little nervous about having someone new in charge.

LDStone: You'll win them over. I'll be waiting. And when I get you alone…

A throat clearing beside her made her jump. Mary Branch stood by the table with a grin on her lined face.

NEKincaid: I'm not alone now, Nadia typed quickly. Her cheeks burned. Must go.

"Is that Mr. Stone?"

LDStone: Tonight.

Nadia closed her laptop with a snap. "Yes."

"I can't wait to meet him. Having him recommend you to us was such a blessing."

An icy finger of unease traced a path down Nadia's spine. *Coincidences happen.*

"Lucas recommended me for this job?"

"Yes. And what a life saver that was since our chairperson had chosen to quit just hours before his phone call."

That icy finger turned into a cold clenched fist.

You're just letting Rand's phone call rattle you. No one is out to get KCL or you.

But Rand's warning echoed in her head. "If he betrayed you once, he'll do it again."

She took a deep breath. "Is there any chance we can get the committee together before dinner instead of after?"

Because she really needed to talk to Lucas and put her mind at ease.

Nadia knew she'd bowled over the committee with the amount of work she'd achieved in one short week.

But she couldn't care less.

Well, okay, yes, she did care. Her success or failure in Dallas depended on her efforts. Not her father's nepotism or his interventions. No one here would pick up after her if she made a mess of her life. And while that was scary in many respects, it was also strangely liberating and empowering. The possibility of failure didn't terrify her the way it would have just a few weeks ago.

But she wanted—no, *needed*—to see Lucas. Her toe tapped impatiently as the elevator inched toward the fiftieth floor.

Lucas had somehow managed to get her the fund-raiser job, but how and why was still a mystery. Mary must have realized she'd leaked something she shouldn't have because she'd clammed up and refused to offer more information when Nadia pressed her.

Finally the elevator doors opened. Nadia surged forward, but jerked to a halt midstep when she nearly crashed into Lucas's housekeeper entering the cubicle.

"Hi, Ella. Is he home yet?" During her nine-week exile she'd become friendly with the woman.

"Hey, Nadia. He is and he's expecting you. Shall I tell him you're here?"

Nadia shifted her laptop case from one slick palm to the other. She hoped talking to Lucas would make the rolling-rocks feeling in her belly go away. "Could you just let me in? I'll surprise him."

Mischief twinkled in Ella's brown eyes. "I guess I can do that. The caterers have already delivered your meal. The hors d'oeuvres are in the refrigerator and dinner is warming in the oven. Dessert's in the freezer and it looks yummy. I've set the table. Mr. Stone said you'd feed yourselves. Would you like for me to come in and pour the wine?"

Nadia followed Ella back to Lucas's door. "I can handle it. But thank you. I know you want to get home to your boys."

"Before they wreck the place and eat everything that isn't fur-covered and meowing." The housekeeper punctuated the sentence with a smile as she turned the key and pushed the panel open. She stepped aside but didn't follow Nadia in.

Ella had the life Nadia had wanted with Lucas. She had three young sons who ran her ragged with their school and sports activities, and Ella and her husband loved every minute of it.

"If you change your mind about me cleaning your apartment, just tell me or Mr. Stone and I'll pop right over."

"Thanks. I will. But I'm determined to show everyone that I can cook and clean for myself. So far, thanks to that list of tips you gave me that first week, I'm winning."

"I understand."

She couldn't possibly. Because Nadia didn't completely understand the postmortem games her father was playing herself. "Have a great night."

"I will. You, too." Ella waved and headed for the elevator.

Nadia let the door close behind her and dropped her satchel next to Lucas's ostrich case beside the hall table. "Lucas?"

Silence greeted her. She checked the living room then the kitchen. Both were empty. She wandered down the hall toward his bedroom, her heels tapping on the hardwood floors. "Lucas?"

When she reached the door the sound of the shower filled her ears. A smile tugged her lips. She should join him.

But after the day she'd had, she'd rather unwind with a glass of wine first. She'd join him after that if he was still showering. She pivoted and headed for the kitchen. She found the corkscrew, opened the Zinfandel and poured a glass. The cool raspberry-flavored liquid rolled easily over her tongue and down her throat.

The man knows his wines.

She took a few more sips, poured a second glass for Lucas then headed for the bedroom. If she wanted to surprise him, she'd have to lose the noisy shoes. She kicked off her sandals by the hall credenza. After another sip of wine, she set down the glasses, peeled her shirt over her head and tossed it onto the glossy cherry surface. The movement set off an avalanche of mail that had been stacked on the far end of the table.

She jumped forward to catch the cascade, but only ended up scattering the pile far and wide. Kneeling, she collected the letters.

Andvari. The familiar name stopped her mid-reach.

The letter was addressed to D. Stone. Andvari, Inc.

D. Stone. *Daniel.*

With shaking hands she gathered the remainder of the mail and, swallowing the bile burning in her throat, she rose on unsteady legs and flipped through the stack of letters. One after the other was addressed to D. Stone, Andvari, Inc.

She hadn't done an Internet search on Daniel Stone. She'd only looked for Lucas Stone.

Lucas had said he owned "a few" companies. Judging by

the volume of mail, Andvari was apparently one of them. And if Andvari owned Teckitron… As if to prove her point, the only letter that hadn't fallen off the table was from Teckitron's CEO.

She wanted to open it and read it to see if it contained information on the purchase of KCL's loans, but another envelope that had slid farther down the hall caught her attention. She took three shaky steps to retrieve it. Her hand stopped inches short and an arctic chill deluged her. The return address was Mardi Gras Cruising.

Dark spots danced in her vision.

Mardi Gras. The company poised to get everything Everett Kincaid owned.

All of KCL's enemies tied to one man. Lucas Daniel Stone.

She had the proof in her hands that this was exactly what Rand had claimed.

A personal vendetta.

Very personal since her position was the one that suffered the most headaches from Andvari's machinations. She had been the one to slog through sleepless nights and eighteen-hour days to find alternative providers for the supplies their cruise ships needed.

But why? Why would Lucas do this?

Her father may have broken up their marriage, but he'd given Lucas two million dollars. Two million that Lucas had apparently multiplied and used to make a very nice life for himself.

If it had been because he'd believed she'd betrayed him eleven years ago, then why up the stakes now and go after the entire company after he'd discovered the truth?

Why would her husband want to destroy her?

Did he hate her that much?

Ten

The shower door flew open.

Startled, Lucas pivoted and opened his eyes.

"Nadia." He'd missed her. More than he wanted to admit.

She stood outside the glass stall half-dressed and entirely too desirable in a skimpy peach-colored bra, a skinny, short skirt in a darker shade and bare feet. He grinned and opened his arms. "Going to join me?"

"You bastard."

The words brought his gaze back to her face. Her furious face. She flung whatever she held in her hands at him. It took him a second to identify the items raining down.

Letters?

He killed the dual shower heads with a twist of his wrist.

An envelope addressed to Mardi Gras circled the drain.

Damn.

She'd found the stack of mail his assistant had left in the

entry for him—a stack he hadn't dealt with yet because he wanted to shower away the jet lag first and he wasn't expecting Nadia for hours. Ella must have let her in.

"Nadia—"

"Don't you dare 'Nadia' me, you lying son of a bitch."

"I can explain."

"How can you explain making my life a living hell? You started eleven years ago and then repeated the process over and over for the past four years and again this week when your stupid company bought up KCL's loans. Did you ever once think of me or were you in this for your own personal gain the entire time? Or is Rand right? Is this a personal vendetta?"

Rand was on to him, too?

"You are a selfish sadistic prick, Lucas Daniel Stone. And it sickens me that I named my son after you."

Her words hit him like a fist to the gut, winding him, making his head spin. He braced a hand against the cool tiles. She'd named their son after him. Knowing that made the loss more real.

She didn't hang around for him to catch his breath or recover his wits. She spun and stalked out of the bathroom.

Stepping over the wet mail, he grabbed a towel from the rod, hitched it around his hips and took off after her. He caught up with her by his front door. She'd put on her shirt, but hadn't tucked it in. One hand held her briefcase and the other clenched the doorknob in a white-knuckled grip. She yanked the door open.

He slapped a palm against the wood slamming it closed again. "Nadia, let me explain."

Although how he'd make her understand the need to destroy her father, or her family in lieu of Everett, escaped him at the moment.

"Get away from me. I don't ever want to see you again." Pure venom dripped from her words. But the quiver in her voice and her bottom lip called her a liar.

He'd hurt her. The knowledge sliced his chest like a knife. He lifted a hand to her cheek. She flinched out of reach and swung her briefcase at him. He dodged and let his hand drop.

"I wasn't trying to hurt you."

"You've done nothing but hurt me. You show me how good something can be then you take it away. And this time, you deliberately set me up. You made love to me and you made me love you all over again. At the same time you were plotting to take everything important to me away. Again."

She loved him. And she wasn't lying. The bruised look in her eyes confirmed her statement. He sucked a breath through the noose squeezing his throat.

"My *vendetta,* as you call it, was against your father. Not you."

"He's dead! And now, so are my feelings for you."

A lie. She'd screamed the words at a spot past his left shoulder.

She had that closed look on her face. But he had to find a way to keep her here until he could fix this. Because he couldn't let her go. Not yet. "What are you going to do? Run back to Miami and hand it all to me on a platter?"

Her spine snapped straight. Her chin hiked and her eyes found and burned his like lasers. "Bastard."

She had no idea how true that was.

"You're better than that, Nadia. Stronger than that. Show me the guts and the smarts of the woman who outmaneuvered me at every turn when I bought up KCL's suppliers. Show me the fighter inside you. I know she's there." His shoulders were so stiff it's a wonder he didn't dislocate something when he feigned a casual shrug. "Unless you're willing to cost your brothers everything."

The color drained from her face. She vibrated with anger and emotion. A white line circled her tight lips. He wouldn't be surprised if she slugged him. "I hope you burn in hell right next to my father."

"Lying in that hospital bed knowing I'd killed our baby, that my wife didn't want me and that I'd probably never walk again was hell. This is playing the game called life. I play to win and I play fair. If I'd wanted to fight dirty, I would have let you sleep past your midnight curfew the night we made love."

"How magnanimous of you." The pain in her eyes made his gut ache. "I lost everything that day, Lucas. The man I loved. Our child and any chance of ever having another one. A month later I learned my mother chose to kill herself rather than stick around and love me. She left me as if I didn't matter. And you did, too.

"I lost everything important—everything money *couldn't* buy. So don't tell me about hell. Or life. Or fighting. Or playing the damned game. I've survived and I've fought and I've done nothing but play the damned game. Because I had to. Or I'd have ended up like my mother. And trust me, there were days when I seriously considered dying the best option. Because I thought I had nothing to live for."

She choked out a mirthless laugh. "But I forgot. You have no conscience. Knowing I spent the better part of four years wishing I'd died in that car with you would have meant nothing to you. You wanted to know why I didn't go to New York and study fashion design? Because I didn't think it mattered what I studied in college. I didn't intend to live long enough to graduate. I was too busy trying to find the nerve to kill myself."

She yanked the door again. In his shock over her words he let her go.

She crossed the hall, shoved her key in her lock and glared at him over her shoulder. "Stay out of my face and out of my way. Or I will take out a restraining order against you so fast you won't know what hit you. And then I'll go to the press and tell them what a mean, selfish, conniving ass you really are."

Her door slammed in his face and the dead bolt shot home as loud as a gun.

Lucas reeled. He braced himself against the doorjamb.

Nadia had considered suicide.

And if she'd ended her life, it would have been his fault.

Trapped.

Nadia curled in a chair in the corner of her patio as far away from Lucas's apartment as she could get. The heavy night air closed around her. Hot. Humid. Suffocating.

She couldn't leave Dallas.

Her brothers were counting on her. The library was counting on her. She was counting on herself. Running from her problems and calling for someone else to bail her out was no longer an option. Her daddy was right. It was time she grew up.

She picked up her cell phone for about the fiftieth time. She had to make the call, but it was the hardest one she'd ever had to make. Calling her brother to tell him she'd screwed up. Again. She'd been betrayed. Again. Used for what she could give someone. Again. No new territory there.

She'd rehashed every conversation she and Lucas had had, picking each sentence apart and trying to decide if she'd given him any crucial, confidential information that would help him in harming KCL. She didn't know.

Taking a bracing breath, she hit Auto-dial.

"Rand Kincaid." He sounded as if she'd woken him.

How late was it? She didn't have a clue. She tipped her head back. The sky overhead was inky dark and star-studded.

"I-It's Nadia. I'm sorry to call so late."

"What's wrong?" Any trace of grogginess in his voice had vanished.

"You were right. It is a personal vendetta. Lucas is behind Andvari and Teckitron and Mardi Gras."

Rand's curses blistered her ears. In the background she heard Tara asking questions and Rand's muffled response. She couldn't make out the words. "Tell me what you know."

She recapped the afternoon's discoveries. Rand didn't rush her. He let her choke out her words. When she was done she sagged against the wall, out of breath, out of energy.

"Nadia, are you okay? I'll charter a jet tonight—"

"No! We're not blowing this or handing that bastard everything. I'm staying here. You're staying there. We're fighting until the end."

"What do you need me to do?"

"Nothing. Just keep on taking care of business the best way you and Mitch can. I'll be fine."

The questions she'd been asking herself since she'd left Lucas's apartment pounded inside her skull.

"Why would he do it, Rand? Why would Dad threaten to leave everything to a man he paid to get out of my life? Why would he choose Lucas over his own children? He had to know who he was dealing with."

"Dad was twisted. It's impossible to make sense out of his actions. But, yes, this seems more whacked than anything I've seen thus far. He detested Stone. Partly because he thought your husband was a fortune hunter and partly because Dad couldn't stand to lose his stranglehold on you."

She blinked and straightened. "Stranglehold?"

"Dad smothered you, Nadia. You reminded him of Mom. You look like her. Your voice and your laugh sound like hers. And you're as artistic as she was."

Rand would know. He'd been fourteen when their mother died, old enough to remember her. Nadia didn't have as many memories. The few she'd had contradicted each other. Sometimes her mother had adored her. Sometimes Mary Elizabeth Kincaid couldn't seem to stand the sight of her youngest child.

"When those bozos tried to kidnap you when you were twelve, Dad went a little crazy. He didn't like letting you out of his sight after that."

"Don't I know it."

"He loved you probably as much as the old bastard was capable of loving anyone."

She hugged the words close. "You think so? Because it didn't feel like it."

"I know so." Rand cleared his throat. "Are you sure you're…okay?"

She knew exactly what he meant. The uncomfortable hesitation was a dead giveaway. He'd been there too many times for her in the past not to know how fragile she'd been in her grief. "I'm fine. I'm not sad or depressed. I'm fighting mad. And Lucas had better not cross me."

"About Stone…"

She clutched her anger around her like a cloak. "Don't worry about him. Now that I know where I stand with him I know how to handle him."

Brave words and a bald-faced lie. But one hint of vulnerability and one or both of her brothers would be in Dallas. And Lucas, the lying snake, would get everything. She couldn't let that happen.

She would figure this out on her own. No calling in the reinforcements. This was her battle and she'd win it on her turf and her terms.

"You have a hell of a nerve showing up here, Stone," Rand Kincaid growled.

Lucas hadn't expected a warm welcome when he reached Kincaid Cruise Line's Miami offices. He'd expected a fist in his face—*if* he'd gotten past security at the reception desk. Judging by the anger vibrating off the Kincaid brothers as they glared at him across the boardroom table he might get a pair of punches before he left the building.

"How is Nadia?"

It had been a damned long two weeks. She'd refused to open her door when he'd knocked and wouldn't speak to him when they passed in the hall. She'd refused the gourmet meals and flowers he'd had delivered.

"None of your goddamned business." Mitch bit out the words.

"The bodyguard is unnecessary. I'm not going to hurt her." One of these turkeys had hired a mountain-size goon to keep him away from her. Nadia never left the apartment without the knuckle-dragger by her side to run interference.

It frustrated him that she lived yards away and couldn't have been more unreachable if she'd been on another continent.

"What do you want?" Rand barked.

"To broker a deal."

The terse curse and redundant hand gesture from the

oldest Kincaid didn't surprise him. Lucas knew his single-minded selfish need for revenge had hurt Nadia deeply. Her brothers wouldn't, and shouldn't, forget that. If she were his sister, he wouldn't.

He hadn't expected making amends and finding a solution or forgiveness to come easily. It had taken him ten days of meetings with a legal team and business advisors to find a potential way around the mess of Everett Kincaid's last wishes.

Neither of the Kincaids invited him to sit.

"My understanding is that if the terms of your father's will aren't met, Mardi Gras cruising becomes the owner of everything he possessed. Correct?"

Rand planted his fists on the table and leaned across aggressively. "How do you know that?"

"Nadia told me part of it. The rest I discovered when I read a copy of Everett's will."

"Son of a bitch," Mitch snarled. "How did you get a copy? It's not public record yet."

"I believe your father's favorite phrase was 'Everyone has a price and a weakness…look hard enough you'll find them.' Everett exploited my weakness and found my price. I was wrong to take his payoff and abandon Nadia. I hurt her. There's no getting around that. My reasons for taking the money don't matter. I make no excuses for being a stupid, greedy coward."

Their raised eyebrows told him he'd shocked them.

"My vendetta was with your father, but as Nadia pointed out, he's gone. It's time to end this. I want to sell Mardi Gras to KCL."

Identical Kincaid chins jacked up. Lucas had Mitch's and Rand's undivided attention. Taking advantage of their stunned silence, he laid his briefcase on the table, popped the locks and withdrew a sheaf of documents. He slid the stack across the wide table and focused on Mitch's eyes—eyes the same green as Nadia's.

"I've had my attorney draw up the sales contract."

"Why?" Rand asked, his tone guarded and suspicious.

"Because if Kincaid Cruise Line owns Mardi Gras Cruising then no matter how this year ends and whether or not the three of you fulfill the terms of Everett's will, KCL and every other property Everett owned will remain in Kincaid hands."

"You're saying if we forfeited, we'd be forfeiting to ourselves. That's twisted logic," Rand said as he flipped through the pages. "But it might work. We'd have to have our attorneys and accountants go over this."

"Of course."

Shaking his head Mitch stepped back from reading over his brother's shoulder. "We can't do it. We don't have the ready cash—as you no doubt know since your company bought off KCL's loans. This is an empty gesture. And if you call the loans, then we're in worse shape than when we started."

"I'm not calling the loans, although I admit that was my initial plan. The terms will remain exactly as stated in the original loan documentation. As for whether or not you can afford the deal…I don't believe you've seen my asking price. Page fifty. Last paragraph."

Pages rustled. Seconds later Rand pinned him with an incredulous stare. "Are you out of your mind?"

"Your father would have sold his entire estate to Mardi Gras—to *me*—for one dollar. It's only fair I match his price."

He'd lose billions. But he'd recover. Because as two long weeks without Nadia had taught him, some things were worth more than money.

Mitch's eyes narrowed to slits. "What's the catch?"

Lucas smiled, because of course there was a catch. There was always a catch when a deal sounded too good to be true.

"Call off the goon. I want to talk to Nadia."

Mitch bristled. "She doesn't want to talk to you."

"That's the deal. I talk to her tonight at the library fund-raiser or the offer is off the table. Take it or leave it."

Mitch still looked ready to punch him, but Rand eyed him with a new respect. "You have one night. After that if she wants nothing to do with you, then you'd better back off."

"Deal." He extended his hand across the table.

Eleven

"You're cutting it close, Cinderella."

Nadia jumped and spun around, nearly falling off her Dolce & Gabbana heels and onto her last year's Badgley Mischka-gowned butt. "Lucas, go away. I don't have time for you now."

She'd been avoiding him for two weeks. Her crazy schedule planning the fund-raiser had helped.

When she'd spotted him in the crowd tonight she'd wanted to run and hide. It hurt to look at him in his black tux and know she'd loved and trusted him twice and each time he'd chosen money over her. But instead of running, she'd simply done her job as MC. Staying onstage had made avoiding him easy.

She scanned the street. Where was the car and driver she'd hired for the night? If she didn't find them soon, she'd have to take a cab…or not. The event had ended fifteen minutes ago and apparently all the taxis had been taken.

"I sent your henchman and your car away," he said as if reading her mind.

"What? You had no right. I need that car. Or is this another ploy to steal my father's estate?"

"Your brothers haven't told you." A statement not a question.

"Told me what?"

"That we talked today."

"You talked to Mitch and Rand? About what?"

He shook his head, an ironic smile twisting his lips. "I'll get you back to your place before midnight. But you'll have to trust me, Nadia."

"Like that's worked so well for me thus far."

"Trust me," he repeated and held her gaze.

She looked into his blue, sincere-looking eyes and called herself an idiot for not telling him to go to hell. She obviously had no judgment where he was concerned. But she didn't run from her problems anymore. She might as well get this confrontation over with.

"Fine. Where's your car?"

He reached for her elbow. She dodged him. He shrugged. "Follow me."

He strolled back toward the building with no apparent haste. After a second she hustled after him. "Lucas, I have to go. I don't have time to hang around here."

"Our ride is on the roof."

"The roof." She stopped.

"The helipad, to be more precise." He opened the glass door and waited for her.

"You flew here in a helicopter?"

"I was out of town today and my flight was delayed. I came here directly from the concourse. There's a helipad on my— our—building."

Car? Helicopter? What did it matter as long as she made it home by midnight? And no matter the mode of transportation, his company would make it an uncomfortable ride. "Let's go."

He led her to the elevator and up to the top floor where they had to depart the cubicle and climb a short flight of stairs. "How did you get permission for this?"

"I made a donation." He shoved open the door to the roof and, sure enough, a small blue-and-white helicopter waited.

"Just like you made a donation to get me the chairperson job."

He looked at her in surprise.

"Did you think I wouldn't find out when I started tallying our take? Money's all that matters to you, isn't it? You're just like my father. The end justifies the means and the bottom line is all that counts."

That stopped him in his tracks. He looked at her. "In my quest for revenge against your father I became so obsessed with humiliating him the way he had me that I became just like him. But I'm not anymore."

She rolled her eyes. "Right. It's so humiliating to take two million dollars."

"He made me beg, dammit," he snapped, then looked away, wiping a hand across his jaw as if he regretted his words. His gaze met hers again. "Everett made sure I knew I was a liability. To you. To my family. He even mentioned getting the police to charge me with involuntary manslaughter in the death of our child. That meant legal fees and possibly jail time. Before he was done with me I was pleading with him to help me."

That sounded like her manipulative father. And okay, yes, she could see how that might sting a man's pride. But to deliberately set out to destroy her family's business…? "Just take me home, Lucas."

He helped her climb aboard—not an easy feat in her long form-fitted gown and heels. His knuckles brushed her belly as he assisted her with her seat belt and her heart jolted with each contact.

Within minutes they were soaring above the Dallas skyline. She'd flown in everything from ultralight planes to jumbo jets, but this helicopter was one of the plushest aircraft she'd ever ridden in. The well-insulated passenger compartment was relatively quiet. The seats were deep and supple leather, the paneling real wood grain.

The jingle of keys pulled her attention back to Lucas. He dangled a pair of keys bearing the Mercedes emblem from his fingers.

"What's that?"

"A gift for you. Congratulations on passing your driving test and getting your license."

She pulled in a shaky breath but ignored the keys. "How did you know?"

"Because I care enough to check. I'm proud of you, Nadia. That took guts."

Her heart hitched and her eyes burned. "Don't. Don't feed me any more lines or lies."

"I'm not."

The cadence of the rotors changed. Nadia used the excuse to break his gaze and look out the window. She hated that she wanted to believe him. She spotted their building and checked her watch. Twenty minutes to spare. Lucas hadn't lied about getting her home on time.

Her stomach lurched as the craft descended then gently bounced on the pad. The motor whined down. Lucas opened the door and handed her out. His palm burned against hers and he refused to release her despite her tug. Her pulse ricocheted wildly as his fingers laced through hers. He said something she couldn't hear to the pilot then guided her toward a door set into the wall.

Moments later she stood in front of her door.

"Invite me in."

She ought to say no. She was exhausted and emotionally wobbly. The past two weeks had been hell. But since he'd given her a ride… "It's been a long day. You can come in for a few minutes."

He followed her into the living room, his eyes scanning the place as if he expected someone to be waiting.

"Do you want a glass of wine or something?" *Some hostess you are. Talk about a rude and abrupt tone…*

He shoved his hands into his jacket pockets. "No. I want to apologize for underestimating you eleven years ago. The truth is, it wasn't you who I thought would fail. It was me. I felt like less than a man. I expected you to reject me so I rejected you first. I was trying to salvage what little pride I had left."

His honesty took her breath. "You were afraid."

His lips compressed then seconds later he nodded. "Terrified. But not half as scared as I was when you told me you'd contemplated suicide. Nadia—"

His voice cracked. He swallowed and blinked. His jaw muscles bunched as if he were gritting his teeth. "I couldn't have lived with that on my conscience."

"I had help. Professional help. And my family."

"You should have had me."

"That would have been nice. We could have helped each other through the tough times."

"You don't ever think about—" He stopped as if he couldn't bear to say the words. She understood his reaction. Most people had the same aversion to the dark side of depression.

"No. Those dark days are over. The doctors believe my issue was a combination of grief and postpartum depression. But I'm okay now. Really okay."

He lifted a hand and stroked her cheek. She felt his touch deep in her belly, but couldn't find the strength to pull away.

"Nadia, I can't go back and undo what I've done wrong. But I will swear to you that I will never underestimate you again. And I will never deliberately make a choice that will hurt you. Give us a second chance. I need you in my life."

The words dredged deeply. A part of her heart yearned to try. But another part held back. Unable to speak past the lump in her throat, she shook her head and moved out of reach.

"My need for revenge is over. I let KCL become symbolic of the pride I surrendered when I took your father's money. I was ashamed. I knew what I'd done was wrong and that I was a coward for not facing you and taking your rejection like a man. I somehow convinced myself while I was battling to get back on my feet that conquering KCL and your father, by humiliating him the way he had me, I could somehow restore the faith I'd lost in myself."

She bit her lip to hold back a hiccup of sympathy. "My father hurt a lot of people."

"He hurt you. I can't forgive him for that."

"But why is he threatening to give you everything if we don't jump through his hoops?"

"I have no idea. The only thing I can guess is that he's been tracking me, monitoring my progress. Maybe he's rewarding me for becoming exactly like the man I despised." He captured her shoulders in his hands. "But I'm not that man anymore. I love you, Nadia. I'm not sure I ever stopped."

She gasped at the swell of emotion his words evoked.

"I love your determination, your persistence, your try-anything-once attitude. But I'm hoping you'll try me. Twice. Give me a second chance to make this right. To make us right."

Her thoughts tumbled like river rocks, rolling over and over noisily. Did she dare trust him again? She wasn't the girl she'd been and could never have the life they'd planned.

Her cell phone rang. She ignored it. But it rang again and again and again.

"Answer it."

She glanced at the caller ID. "It's Rand. I'll call him back."

"Answer it," he repeated more insistently.

"What?" she practically barked into the phone.

"Are you with Stone?"

She blinked. "Yes. Why?"

"Give the man a dollar and tell him he has a deal."

"What?"

"Just do it, Nadia. He'll explain." Rand hung up on her.

She stared at the phone. "That was weird. He said, 'Give the man a dollar and tell him he has a deal.' What does that mean?"

A smile slid across Lucas's sexy lips. "Need to borrow a dollar?"

"I have a dollar. But why would I give it to you?"

He held out his hand, palm up.

Grunting in frustration, Nadia dug a dollar out of her evening bag and slapped it into his hand. Hard.

He tucked it into his pant pocket. "I flew to Miami today to broker a deal with your brothers."

Suspicious, she narrowed her eyes. "What kind of deal?"

"KCL now owns Mardi Gras Cruising or will as soon as the paperwork is signed and notarized."

"What?"

"KCL bought Mardi Gras for one dollar—the price your father put on his holdings. When the deal is closed you can get out of this apartment and go anywhere you want. You'll be free instead of trapped here for a year."

"I don't understand. Why would you sell your company at a multibillion-dollar loss? What's in it for you?" None of this made sense. Just two weeks ago Lucas had been trying to destroy KCL.

"What's that old cliché? When you love someone you let them go? You won't be bound by the terms of your father's will because if you forfeit, everything will be handed over to Mardi Gras, which you Kincaids will already own. So you'll be giving it to yourselves."

The convoluted logic almost made sense. "Is that legal?"

"According to the best legal minds I could buy, yes. And I'm sure your brothers had their attorneys go through the purchase agreement with a fine-tooth comb, too, before agreeing."

"You sold your company for a dollar so I could have my freedom?"

"I want you to be happy, Nadia. With or without me. That's all I ever wanted. Even when I walked away eleven years ago that was my goal."

Her vision clouded. She blinked to clear the tears and a hot trail burned down her cheek. "I'll stay in Dallas for the full year because Daddy expected me to fail. I need to prove to him and to myself that I can take whatever life dishes out."

"Now that's the attitude of the woman who's given Andvari hell for the past forty months."

"I'm not the girl you fell in love with eleven years ago, Lucas. I can't give you the family you want. I can't have children."

"We don't have to make babies to be happy together."

"I don't even know if I want to risk adopting. The doctors tell me I don't carry my mother's trait for bipolar disorder. But what if they're wrong? What if I end up ill?"

"You said I never gave you a chance to prove your love for me by telling you I was paralyzed. Works both ways, princess. You're not giving me a chance to prove mine, either. Nadia, I will love you even if you end up like your mother. And if you need it, then I will take care of you and keep you safe to the best of my ability." He cradled her face in his palms. "I love you. Let me prove it."

And then his lips touched hers in the gentlest kiss they'd ever shared. When he lifted his head she looked into his eyes and saw the emotion to mirror his words. Her heart swelled and tears of happiness clogged her throat.

She covered his hands with hers. "I want to take that chance. With you. Only with you."

"Marry me."

She gave him a patient look. "I'm already married to you."

"Marry me again. But this time we'll meet at the altar as equals."

"I never considered you less than my equal, Lucas. But if it's important to you, then, yes, I'll marry you again."

Epilogue

Nadia sat behind her desk at KCL and sighed in satisfaction. It was good to be home and back on the job.

Her year in exile had flown by—thanks to Lucas's company—and life was good.

No, better than good because she had it all this time. A husband who adored her. A job she loved. And family. His and hers.

She glanced at the card that had been tucked in the massive flower arrangement from Lucas's mother and sisters.

Party at 7:00 to celebrate your first day back on the job.
Be ready to boogie Stone-style. Martinis on us.
Lucas's Girls

"Ms. Kinc—Mrs. Stone, your husband is here," her assistant said over the intercom.

"Send him in, Ann." She rose, circled her desk to meet him halfway.

Lucas strode through the door, looking powerful and gorgeous as always, this time in her favorite black Armani suit. His blond hair gleamed, but it was the way his eyes lit up when he saw her that made her heart flip-flop. Not once in the past nine months had she had any reason to doubt his love or his loyalty.

He covered the carpet in long strides and didn't stop until his arms surrounded her and his lips covered hers. She adored his kisses. The devouring ones, the gentle ones, the tempting ones, but she especially liked this kind—the kind that promised more than kisses later.

He lifted his head. "Good first day back?"

"Absolutely." When he kissed her breathless that way she couldn't expect long-winded answers. He was lucky to get more than one syllable.

"Ready for this?" The sun glinted off his wedding band— the one she'd given him years ago—as he reached into his coat pocket and withdrew an envelope.

The final words from her father. Her heart stumbled.

Each of her brothers had received letters from her father soon after completing their portions of the yearlong inheritance clause. It stood to reason she'd get one, too. Lucas had volunteered to pick hers up from Richards's office on his way back from the final inspection of the property he'd purchased to house all of his businesses in Miami. Mardi Gras would fall under the KCL umbrella, but his other companies would be housed near enough that she and he could slip away for lunches together.

"Would you rather do this at home?" he asked.

She shook her head. "No. I want to read Dad's words here

where I can still feel his presence. He may have broken us up, but he also brought us back together. And I'd have to be in serious denial not to admit that we're both stronger people for difficulties we went through and the time we spent apart."

"Agreed. But I still resent being robbed of eleven years with you." He offered her an envelope, which left one in his hand.

"He left me two letters?"

He shook his head, a frown puckering his brow. "Your father left one for me."

"That's odd. I don't think anyone else outside the family received a last missive."

"Who goes first?" he asked.

"Me. I need answers." She led him to what she called her oasis, a seating nook in the corner of her office. Lucas had helped her build a minigarden when she'd moved in over the weekend. She had blooming orchids mixed in with the emerald-green tropical plants and fragrant gardenias. She kicked off her Versace heels and sat on the love seat. Lucas settled beside her, hooking his arm around her shoulder and tugging her close.

Nadia's hands trembled as she opened the flap and withdrew the folded pages. She took a deep breath and flattened the pages in her lap so that Lucas could read along with her.

Nadia,
    If you're reading this, then you have passed the final test your old man is going to throw at you, and I'm probably exactly where you've told me to go a hundred times. Roasting in hell. I'm not saying I didn't deserve the verbal fireballs when you threw them. I held you too tight.

My only excuse—well, I have two of them. First, your mother, my darling Mary Elizabeth, made me promise to take care of her little angel. (Almost blew that one, didn't I?) I think she knew she wouldn't be around to do the job. But don't ever doubt she loved you. She just couldn't fight her demons. And God help me, I couldn't fight them for her even though I tried.

Second, you reminded me of your mother in so many ways. Your laugh. Your smile. Your zest for life and your artistic talent. Although you're mentally much stronger than she ever was. I barely survived losing her. I didn't think I'd survive losing you, too. But I almost did lose you. And it was my own stupid fault.

In protecting you from life's lows, I also robbed you of life's highs. I can't help believing if I'd given you the wedding your mother would have wanted you to have complete with chauffeurs and horse-drawn carriages, then you wouldn't have lost my first grandson. And you wouldn't have hit rock bottom. That guilt ate away at me every blessed day. And I made things worse by getting rid of Stone.

I was wrong about him, Nadia. And you know how much it sticks in my craw to admit to being wrong. But I shouldn't have tried to play God. He loved you and I had no right to take that from you. But I did. I shamelessly kicked the man when he was down and bleeding. Literally. When I look back on my life, that is not one of my finer moments and it is my biggest regret. In trying to make your life easier, I robbed you of the love of your life and denied you the chance to experience what I had with your mother. As much as losing her hurt me, I would do it all again to relive the days I had with her.

Sending you to Dallas where you'd run into Stone may have been too little too late. But I had to try. And I hate like hell that I won't be around to see the outcome.

If nothing else, I hope this year on your own has shown you your inner strength. You always were a fighter. The only Kincaid who fought as hard and tough as me. That's why seeing you so down after the accident gutted me. And, yes, I pushed you around and hit your hot buttons just to get a rise out of you. But it beat the hell out of watching you go through the motions without caring what happened. (Boy, did you make me pay for hitting your buttons.)

If this letter finds Stone by your side, then I wish the two of you years of happiness and joy, and I take credit for fixing my biggest mistake and getting you back together. If he's not with you, then he's not the man I thought he was and he's not worthy of you. Screw him.

But you're a stubborn cuss, just like your old man. If he's not there and you want him, I'll hand you one last weapon. You're still married to him. The divorce paperwork was forged. I've left a letter with Richards saying so. Again, my intentions were good but maybe my methods weren't the best. If either you or he had wanted to marry again, I'd have had a hell of a mess on my hands. But I figured since that kind of love only comes once in a lifetime, I was pretty safe.

Two pieces of advice to you, Nadia… First, remember if you don't believe in yourself no one else will. I hope this year gave you that confidence. And second, live life to the fullest—the good and the bad—before you run out of time and all you have are regrets for what you didn't do and things you didn't say. Like I did.

I never told you I loved you. Now I'll never get the chance except in cold, dry words typed on paper. Too little. Too late.

I love you, baby girl. And I am so damned proud of you. Your mother would have been, too. You are easily the best thing Mary Elizabeth and I ever did together and the best parts of both of us combined.

Your father,
Everett Kincaid

Nadia blinked furiously to clear her vision. A blur of white passed in front of her eyes. Lucas's handkerchief. She'd become quite fond of those little white monogrammed squares and the games they played with them over the past months.

She accepted it and blotted her wet face. "My mother and father loved me. You can't know how many times I wondered."

Lucas's arm tightened around her. "I told you it was impossible not to love you, princess."

"But Daddy didn't explain that clause concerning Mardi Gras. Why would he choose you over his own children?"

"Maybe my letter has the answer." He opened the envelope and withdrew a single sheet.

Stone,

I wronged each of my children. But I wronged you even more. And in doing so, I almost lost my daughter.

Ironic, isn't it? In trying to crush you I almost destroyed the person who meant the world to me, my baby girl, the spitting image of my Mary Elizabeth and the apple of her mother's eye.

I've followed your progress over the years. I guess I was hoping you'd prove I'd done the right thing in getting rid of your ass. But you didn't. You made me eat crow every time I turned around. Not my favorite diet, I'll tell you.

Stone, you have more chutzpah than me. Honest to God, I don't know another person I can say that to. Your ambition and intelligence remind me of myself at your age. But you're smarter, more patient. And since your good-for-nothing father (yes, I know about the bastard) isn't around to say it, let me say it. You are one hell of a man. Remember, it's not who your daddy is that matters. It's who you are that counts.

In putting your family first (hell yes, I know why you took my money), you showed me my mistake in tearing you and Nadia apart. But I was stubborn. I stuck to my guns. And then you multiplied *my* money and turned around and used it against me. Damnation, man, that takes balls. My hat is off to you.

I have no doubt that if I hadn't been watching you like a hawk you would have eventually launched a sneak attack on KCL and taken us down. I've made enough mistakes to give you footholds. You're good. Since I wasn't going to be around to see it happen I decided I'd reward you for your cunning. But I won't deny I'm hoping my kids have enough of me in them to spike your guns.

Gotta love a good fair fight.

If you learned the terms of my will (and I'm sure you did), you know how easily you could have won by cheating. If you're reading this, then you played straight. I gave you a second chance to choose between my money and my daughter. You did the right thing. I have to respect a man whose moral code is strong enough to keep him from taking the easy road.

I didn't play fair with you last time, Stone, and for that I apologize. You'll notice I did this time. I didn't give my family advance warning of your identity and your intent. To the victor goes the spoils and all that crap.

I sure did love watching you and Nadia sparring with that Andvari mess. Proved to me once and for all that the two of you were evenly matched. Good God, that girl has what my daddy called gumption. Stuck it to you, didn't she? It was a pure joy to watch the two of you dancing around the ring.

I wish I could be around to see how this battle ends, because I'll bet it's going to be one hell of a show.

Take care of my daughter, Stone. Love her and any children you might adopt until your last breath. If you don't, I'm going to come back and haunt your ass.

Respectfully yours,
Everett Kincaid

The last line of the letter startled a burst of laughter from Nadia. She blotted more tears, but she was smiling. "That sounds exactly like my father."

"He knew it was me the entire time."

Only one line of the letter bothered her. "He thinks we're going to adopt."

"Princess, I'm happy with just you."

"We always wanted a family. You'd be such a good father."

"Then we'll get goldfish or dogs."

She took a deep breath, rolling the words she'd been privately thinking around in her head. "I—I think I'd like to raise children with you."

His sharp breath told him she'd surprised him.

She worried her bottom lip with her teeth. "Maybe we could hire a surrogate to carry your baby. Or check into adoption."

He stroked her cheek with a gentle hand, but it was the love in his eyes that cocooned her. "We'll do whatever you want. But remember, as long as I have you I have all I need."

* * * * *

Turn the page for a sneak preview of
AFTERSHOCK, *a new anthology*
featuring New York Times *bestselling author*
Sharon Sala.

Available October 2008.

n●cturne™

Dramatic and sensual tales of paranormal romance.

Chapter 1

October
New York City

Nicole Masters was sitting cross-legged on her sofa while a cold autumn rain peppered the windows of her fourth-floor apartment. She was poking at the ice cream in her bowl and trying not to be in a mood.

Six weeks ago, a simple trip to her neighborhood pharmacy had turned into a nightmare. She'd walked into the middle of a robbery. She never even saw the man who shot her in the head and left her for dead. She'd survived, but some of her senses had not. She was dealing with short-term memory loss and a tendency to stagger. Even though she'd been told the problems were most likely temporary, she waged a daily battle with depression.

Her parents had been killed in a car wreck when she was twenty-one. And except for a few friends—and most recently her boyfriend, Dominic Tucci, who lived in the apartment right above hers, she was alone. Her doctor kept reminding her that she should be grateful to be alive, and on one level she knew he was right. But he wasn't living in her shoes.

If she'd been anywhere else but at that pharmacy when the robbery happened, she wouldn't have died twice on the way to the hospital. Instead of being grateful that she'd survived, she couldn't stop thinking of what she'd lost.

But that wasn't the end of her troubles. On top of everything else, something strange was happening inside her head. She'd begun to hear odd things: sounds, not voices—at least, she didn't think it was voices. It was more like the distant noise of rapids—a rush of wind and water inside her head that, when it came, blocked out everything around her. It didn't happen often, but when it did, it was frightening, and it was driving her crazy.

The blank moments, which is what she called them, even had a rhythm. First there came that sound, then a cold sweat, then panic with no reason. Part of her feared it was the beginning of an emotional breakdown. And part of her feared it wasn't—that it was going to turn out to be a permanent souvenir of her resurrection.

Frustrated with herself and the situation as it stood, she upped the sound on the TV remote. But instead of *Wheel of Fortune,* an announcer broke in with a special bulletin.

"This just in. Police are on the scene of a kidnapping that occurred only hours ago at The Dakota. Molly Dane, the six-year-old daughter of one of Hollywood's blockbuster stars, Lyla Dane, was taken by force from the family apartment. At this time they have yet to receive a ransom demand. The housekeeper was seriously injured during the abduction, and is, at the present time, in surgery. Police are hoping to be able to talk to her once she regains consciousness. In the meantime, we are going now to a press conference with Lyla Dane."

Horrified, Nicole stilled as the cameras went live to where the actress was speaking before a bank of microphones. The shock and terror in Lyla Dane's voice were physically painful to watch. But even though Nicole kept upping the volume, the sound continued to fade.

Just when she was beginning to think something was wrong with her set, the broadcast suddenly switched from the Dane press conference to what appeared to be footage of the kidnapping, beginning with footage from inside the apartment.

When the front door suddenly flew back against the wall and four men rushed in, Nicole gasped. Horrified, she quickly realized that this must have been caught on a security camera inside the Dane apartment.

As Nicole continued to watch, a small Asian woman, who she guessed was the maid, rushed forward in an effort to keep them out. When one of the men hit her in the face with his gun, Nicole moaned. The violence was too reminiscent of what she'd lived through. Sick to her stomach, she fisted her hands against her belly, wishing it was over, but unable to tear her gaze away.

When the maid dropped to the carpet, the same man followed with a vicious kick to the little woman's midsection that lifted her off the floor.

"Oh, my God," Nicole said. When blood began to pool beneath the maid's head, she started to cry.

As the tape played on, the four men split up in different

directions. The camera caught one running down a long marble hallway, then disappearing into a room. Moments later he reappeared, carrying a little girl, who Nicole assumed was Molly Dane. The child was wearing a pair of red pants and a white turtleneck sweater, and her hair was partially blocking her abductor's face as he carried her down the hall. She was kicking and screaming in his arms, and when he slapped her, it elicited an agonized scream that brought the other three running. Nicole watched in horror as one of them ran up and put his hand over Molly's face. Seconds later, she went limp.

One moment they were in the foyer, then they were gone.

Nicole jumped to her feet, then staggered drunkenly. The bowl of ice cream she'd absentmindedly placed in her lap shattered at her feet, splattering glass and melting ice cream everywhere.

The picture on the screen abruptly switched from the kidnapping to what Nicole assumed was a rerun of Lyla Dane's plea for her daughter's safe return, but she was numb.

Before she could think what to do next, the doorbell rang. Startled by the unexpected sound, she shakily swiped at the tears and took a step forward. She didn't feel the glass shards piercing her feet until she took the second step. At that point, sharp pains shot through her foot. She gasped, then looked down in confusion. Her legs looked as if she'd been running through mud, and she was standing in broken glass and ice cream, while a thin ribbon of blood seeped out from beneath her toes.

"Oh, no," Nicole mumbled, then stifled a second moan of pain.

The doorbell rang again. She shivered, then clutched her head in confusion.

"Just a minute!" she yelled, then tried to sidestep the rest of the debris as she hobbled to the door.

When she looked through the peephole in the door, she didn't know whether to be relieved or regretful.

It was Dominic, and as usual, she was a mess.

Nicole smiled a little self-consciously as she opened the door to let him in. "I just don't know what's happening to me. I think I'm losing my mind."

"Hey, don't talk about my woman like that."

Nicole rode the surge of delight his words brought. "So I'm still your woman?"

Dominic lowered his head.

Their lips met.

The kiss proceeded.

Slowly.

Thoroughly.

* * * * *

Be sure to look for the
AFTERSHOCK *anthology next month, as*
well as other exciting paranormal stories
from Silhouette Nocturne.
Available in October wherever books are sold.

nocturne™

NEW YORK TIMES BESTSELLING AUTHOR

SHARON SALA

JANIS REAMES HUDSON
DEBRA COWAN

AFTERSHOCK

Three women are brought to the brink of death...
only to discover the aftershock of their trauma has
left them with unexpected and unwelcome gifts of
paranormal powers. Now each woman must learn to
accept her newfound abilities while fighting for life,
love and second chances....

Available October wherever books are sold.

www.eHarlequin.com
www.paranormalromanceblog.wordpress.com   SN61796

REQUEST YOUR FREE BOOKS!

2 FREE NOVELS PLUS 2 FREE GIFTS!

Passionate, Powerful, Provocative!

YES! Please send me 2 FREE Silhouette Desire® novels and my 2 FREE gifts (gifts are worth about $10). After receiving them, if I don't wish to receive any more books, I can return the shipping statement marked "cancel". If I don't cancel, I will receive 6 brand-new novels every month and be billed just $4.05 per book in the U.S. or $4.74 per book in Canada, plus 25¢ shipping and handling per book and applicable taxes, if any*. That's a savings of almost 15% off the cover price! I understand that accepting the 2 free books and gifts places me under no obligation to buy anything. I can always return a shipment and cancel at any time. Even if I never buy another book, the two free books and gifts are mine to keep forever.

225 SDN ERVX 326 SDN ERVM

Name	(PLEASE PRINT)	

Address		Apt. #

City	State/Prov.	Zip/Postal Code

Signature (if under 18, a parent or guardian must sign)

Mail to the **Silhouette Reader Service:**
IN U.S.A.: P.O. Box 1867, Buffalo, NY 14240-1867
IN CANADA: P.O. Box 609, Fort Erie, Ontario L2A 5X3

Not valid to current subscribers of Silhouette Desire books.

Want to try two free books from another line?
Call 1-800-873-8635 or visit www.morefreebooks.com.

* Terms and prices subject to change without notice. N.Y. residents add applicable sales tax. Canadian residents will be charged applicable provincial taxes and GST. Offer not valid in Quebec. This offer is limited to one order per household. All orders subject to approval. Credit or debit balances in a customer's account(s) may be offset by any other outstanding balance owed by or to the customer. Please allow 4 to 6 weeks for delivery. Offer available while quantities last.

Your Privacy: Silhouette Books is committed to protecting your privacy. Our Privacy Policy is available online at www.eHarlequin.com or upon request from the Reader Service. From time to time we make our lists of customers available to reputable third parties who may have a product or service of interest to you. If you would prefer we not share your name and address, please check here. ☐

SDES08R

Silhouette®

Romantic
SUSPENSE

**Sparked by Danger,
Fueled by Passion.**

USA TODAY bestselling author

Merline Lovelace

Undercover Wife

Secret agent Mike Callahan, code name Hawkeye,
objects when he's paired with sophisticated
Gillian Ridgeway on a dangerous spy mission
to Hong Kong. Gillian has secretly been in love
with him for years, but Hawk is an overprotective
man with a wounded past that threatens to
resurface. Now the two must put their lives—
and hearts—at risk for each other.

Available October wherever books are sold.

COMING NEXT MONTH

#1897 MARRIAGE, MANHATTAN STYLE—Barbara Dunlop
Park Avenue Scandals
Secrets, blackmail and infertility had their marriage on the rocks.
Will an unexpected opportunity at parenthood give them a second
chance?

#1898 THE MONEY MAN'S SEDUCTION—Leslie LaFoy
Gifts from a Billionaire
Suspicious of her true motives, he vows to keep her close—but as
close as in his bed?

#1899 DANTE'S CONTRACT MARRIAGE—Day Leclaire
The Dante Legacy
Forced to marry to protect an infamous diamond, they never
counted on being struck by The Dante Inferno. Suddenly their
convenient marriage is full of *in*convenient passion.

#1900 AN AFFAIR WITH THE PRINCESS—Michelle Celmer
Royal Seductions
He'd had an affair with the princess, once upon a time. But why
had he returned? Remembrance…or revenge?

#1901 MISTAKEN MISTRESS—Tessa Radley
The Saxon Brides
Could this woman he feels such a reckless passion for really be
his late brother's mistress? Or are there other secrets she's hiding?

#1902 BABY BENEFITS—Emily McKay
Billionaires and Babies
Her boss had a baby—and he needed her help. How could she
possibly deny him…how could she ever resist him?